Alex Mabon was born in Inverness at the outbreak of the Second World War. On leaving school he had a spell in journalism before enlisting in the Royal Air Force where he spent ten years, mainly in the Middle East and the Far East. Following a career in commercial property and business continuity management in the City of London, he retired. He lives in Kent with his wife Denise.

www.alexmabon.co.uk

By the same author.

The Lads from the Ferry
Published 2004 ***(Vanguard)***
ISBN 184386 129 1

The Battle of the Ferry
Published 2005 ***(Pegasus)***
ISBN 190349 016 2

The Boy who saved the World
Published 2006 ***(Nightingale)***
ISBN 190349 138 X

MURDER DOWN THE MEDWAY

Alex Mabon

Murder Down The Medway

Pegasus

PEGASUS PAPERBACK

© Copyright 2006
Alex Mabon

The right of Alex Mabon to be identified as author of
this work has been asserted by him in accordance with the
Copyright, Designs and Patents Act 1988

All Rights Reserved

No reproduction, copy or transmission of this publication
may be made without written permission.
No paragraph of this publication may be reproduced,
copied or transmitted save with the written permission of the
publisher, or in accordance with the provisions
of the Copyright Act 1956 (as amended).

Any person who does any unauthorised act in relation to
this publication may be liable to criminal
prosecution and civil claims for damage.

A CIP catalogue record for this title is
available from the British Library

ISBN 1 903490 227

Pegasus is an imprint of
Pegasus Elliot MacKenzie Publishers Ltd.
www.pegasuspublishers.com

First Published in 2006

Pegasus
Sheraton House Castle Park
Cambridge England

Printed & Bound in Great Britain

This book is dedicated to the memory of

Elizabeth Kerr Smith MacRae
A true Scots lass

Iris Millicent Slattery
A true Medway lass

PROLOGUE

May 1947

The young boy curled into the foetal position and pulled the pillow over his ears. The shouting had begun the moment his father had entered the house. He could hear the raised voices – his father shouting, his mother pleading.

He heard the sound of a fist connecting with flesh and closed his eyes, in the vain hope that this action would erase the sounds.

A deep silence came over the house. He held his breath, knowing what was to happen next. He whimpered as he heard the heavy footsteps on the staircase. The bedroom door creaked. The smell of alcohol was over-powering. He shuddered involuntarily as the bedcovers were pulled back to reveal his small body.

The boy was dragged out of bed. His pale limbs stood out against the dinginess of his surroundings.

"Please God, let him die, take my father away from me."

The prayer ran through the boy's mind, in an attempt to erase the pain.

***

The young child stared at the small coffin. It was heartbreaking to lose a younger sister. Picking up the kitten, the child vowed that one day, no matter how long it took, the person responsible for her death would be punished.

CHAPTER ONE

Chatham, April 1963

Donnie Grey pulled himself up to his full height and gazed into the mirror. At six foot two inches in height, and weighing fifteen stone, he was a handsome figure of a man. At the age of twenty three he had the women of Chatham, young and old, at his beck and call. Glancing once again in the mirror, he brushed back his Elvis quiff. Wearing a three quarter length black jacket with velvet collar and velvet pockets, drainpipe trousers, and brothel creeper shoes, he looked what he was – a fashionably dressed thug on the pull. He may have missed the original teddy-boy era by several years, but this did not bother Donnie. He wore what he wanted to wear. The men of Chatham who made adverse comment on Donnie's dress sense, usually when they had too much to drink, had cause to regret it.

Donnie had been in The Eagle Tavern for half an hour when Andy Spiers turned up. Andy was the product of a gambling father and a drunken slut of a mother. Dressed in his normal attire, a dark suit with a dark tie, Andy gave Donnie a brief nod as he entered the pub. Donnie was surprised to see Ann Stanton with Andy as the last time he had seen her was the previous summer, just before she had been sentenced to six months imprisonment for assaulting a policeman who had arrested her for soliciting. Ann Stanton had a wild reputation.

Five minutes after Andy entered the public house, drugs exchanged hands. Andy was an established seller. Donnie was an apprentice in the craft.

Chatham born and bred, Donnie came from a broken home. The small two up two down terraced house in the back streets of the town, close to the railway station, was run down and derelict. Donnie's parents were dead. He had become a loose cannon since their death eight months previously. Donnie's future in the world was fairly predictable.

Donnie picked up his pint of stout and mild. He may have been a novice in the drug world, but he was already a connoisseur of alcohol.

He tapped his fingers on the table and looked around the public bar. The floor was covered in sawdust. Beer spillage had already turned the sawdust into mush in one area of the bar. Blood would no doubt be added to the mixture before closing time. A group of sailors from Chatham Naval Base were seated in one corner of the squalid room. Three squaddies from Brompton Barracks stood at the bar. Donnie knew, with certainty, that within the hour, a fight would break out between the servicemen.

Two tired looking women, in their mid forties, but wearing mini-skirts, stiletto heels, and enough make-up to keep Max Factor in profit for a year, sat staring at the servicemen. It was seven o'clock in the evening. The girls had a long night ahead of them.

At a corner table, nursing a glass of brown ale, and oblivious to everything but the juke-box, sat a diminutive lonely figure of a man. He was about the same age as Donnie, but miles apart in stature.

Donnie stood up. He had visits to make. He had three prospective customers. With a mark up of three hundred percent Donnie would do well. The money he made as a storeman in the dockyard clothing store was peanuts compared to what he would make passing drugs.

Donnie reflected on the whispered proposition that had been made by Andy on passing over the drugs. Through working in the dockyard Donnie was in a position to receive drugs as they were smuggled into the country on Royal Navy ships. All Donnie had to do was to get them out of the dockyard.

It took Donnie one minute to agree to Andy's proposition.

He knew exactly how to get the drugs past the Admiralty police at Pembroke gate.

Whistling cheerfully as he left The Eagle, Donnie made his way to the bus-station. He had an evening planned at the Invicta Ballroom. With Duke D'mond and The Barron Knights on the bill, a good night was assured. And, after the dance, he would invite some lucky girl for a walk down the Strand at Gillingham.

CHAPTER TWO

Chatham, April 1963

A week after Donnie Grey's meeting with Andy Spiers in The Eagle, agreement was reached between the two men, on how the drug trafficking would operate.

Three weeks passed before Donnie spoke to Andy again. The following day he met with a Royal Navy petty officer. A package exchanged hands.

In the safety of a locked storeroom in the dockyard, Donnie opened the package. The package contained several hundred small sachets of white pills.

When eight hundred cyclists exited Chatham dockyard via Pembroke Gate at end of work that day, Donnie Grey was in the middle group of cyclists. A random check was made by the Admiralty police. Donnie's foreman, in the lead group of cyclists, was stopped. Donnie laughed as he looked over his shoulder and saw the irate foreman having his lunch-bag checked.

Five minutes after arriving at his home Donnie removed the saddle and handlebars from his bicycle. Stuffed into the frame of the bicycle were the smuggled drugs.

That evening Donnie met Andy in The Bull public house. In the lounge bar of the Military Road hostelry the drugs were handed over. Andy advised Donnie that he had an even more lucrative source of supply. Donnie could be part of that as well.

Donnie Grey had taken a big step on a slippery slope. The die determining the course of his life had been firmly cast.

The following day Donnie reached a decision. He had a long standing score to settle. Somebody had to be punished. It was the least he could do for his sister.

CHAPTER THREE

Maidstone, May 1963

The cocktail bar in the Star Hotel was crowded, despite being the most expensive lodging house in the Maidstone area.

Dressed in sports jacket and slacks, Petty Officer John Piper was holding court. His attentive audience, two attractive women of questionable drinking age, were listening intently, enthralled by his tales of life in foreign ports.

Piper broke off from his impressive chat-up line to catch the eye of a passing waiter. The waiter acknowledged his gesture. Two minutes later a fresh bottle of champagne was placed in the ice bucket. The naval officer knew how to enjoy his shore leave.

***

Ted Ashcroft, a long serving inspector with the Admiralty police, with special responsibility for major crimes perpetrated in the area of naval dockyards, watched John Piper pouring the champagne. During the hour he had been watching the petty officer, three bottles of champagne had been drunk. The cost of the champagne was equivalent to one month's wages for the petty officer.

The investigation into the activities of Piper had begun nine months earlier. The investigation was instigated when Piper had been seen in the foyer of the five star Surrey Hotel in London's Park Lane with a known drug dealer. A police surveillance of the hotel had been underway at the time. A check of the hotel records showed that Piper had booked into the hotel for two nights. When the Metropolitan Police enquires on Piper's background revealed that he was a naval petty officer their suspicions were aroused. There was no way that Piper could afford to stay at the Surrey Hotel on a petty officer's salary. The Met referred the matter to the Royal Navy. The service police took the decision to keep quiet. Petty Officer Piper had no idea that the Admiralty Police and Scotland Yard had him under surveillance.

Piper had been followed from the moment he had stepped ashore in Chatham dockyard the previous week, but nothing suspicious had been seen. On leaving his ship he had visited the dockyard pay office and the clothing store, where he requisitioned a new uniform. He had then re-boarded his ship. He had left the dockyard the previous day, and had booked into the Star Hotel. Apart from obvious signs of an expensive lifestyle, nothing untoward had occurred. A discreet check of his bank account revealed that he had more than five thousand pounds in savings.

Ted Ashcroft knew that Piper was smuggling drugs into the country. What he could not figure out was how Piper was disposing of the drugs. He decided that it was time for him to report back to the Met Police.

The Met responded by asking the Admiralty police to take no action. They already knew who Piper's contacts were in the Medway towns.

CHAPTER FOUR

London, June 1963

Detective Inspector Fred Goodall glanced out of the window of the Central Drugs Squad office located on the sixteenth floor of New Scotland Yard. Outside the sun glistened on Westminster Abbey. Big Ben tolled in the background. Goodall checked his watch. It was midday.

Detective Constable Ted Williams from the Kent Constabulary, dressed in a smart, beige coloured, lightweight summer suit, looked around the small meeting room. It was his first visit to New Scotland Yard. He was not sure what to expect, when he had been instructed to attend a meeting there by his Chief Superintendent at Chatham Police Station. He certainly had not expected to be confronted by a bunch of drop-outs.

Fred Goodall glanced around the room. Despite the warm summer's day he was dressed in a Hells Angel leather jacket and jeans, and sported a pony tail. In his late thirties, he had all the appearance of a non-conformist to rules and regulations.

"Is Billy around?" he asked.

A tall skinhead, with tattoos on his forearms, nodded his head. "He's just getting the coffee, boss."

At that moment the door to the briefing room opened. A tall well-built man in his mid-twenties entered the room. He was precariously balancing three paper cups. He kicked the door behind him as he entered the room.

"I hope one of these is for me."

"Of course boss. Hope I haven't held things up" replied Billy Saunders, in a soft Scottish voice.

"No. Take a seat, and we'll get started."

Billy Saunders, dressed in a leather jacket and sporting a

small beard and earrings, casually dropped into a chair.

"Right, simmer down everybody. You all know who I am. I'll leave you to do your own introductions later on. My objective here is to brief you on the planned raid on the drugs factory in Eleanor Road, Plaistow. We have had the place under surveillance for over three months. We know that large quantities of amphetamines are being produced there, and these are being distributed throughout Kent and Essex. The respective forces from these counties will have responsibility for picking up the dealers in their area. The Met Police team, comprising myself, Detective Constable Riley and Detective Constable Jacobs, will have responsibility for the raid on the factory. We will have the back up of an armed unit. Detective Constable Billy Saunders will liaise with the Kent force, and Detective Constable David Robson with the Essex force."

Thirty minutes later Fred Goodall finished his briefing.

***

Billy Saunders took ten minutes to explain to Ted Williams what was required from the Kent Constabulary. "So you reckon the turnover of this factory is six million quid a year."

"That's just a conservative estimate."

"And the Kent force has to arrest the pushers at the same time as the Met raid the factory."

"That's it. Here is the list of names. It covers most of the county. I'll be with you co-ordinating the arrests. It's important that we pick them all up at the same time."

CHAPTER FIVE

Inverness, June 1963

"I've got some bad news for you Billy. I'm afraid that your father has been taken ill. It sounds quite serious."

"I'll get home straight away boss. I should be back in a couple of days."

The conversation between Billy Saunders and Fred Goodall had taken place four days earlier. Eight hours later Billy Saunders arrived in Inverness. Two hours after his arrival his father passed away.

The funeral service for Tom Saunders was well attended. He had worked as a compositor on a local newspaper for most of his working life. He had raised Billy on his own after losing his wife to pneumonia when Billy was still a child. Tom Saunders had been proud of his son.

"Sorry about your loss, he was a good man. He always had time for a chat. He never quite got over the loss of your mother."

Billy Saunders, more appropriately dressed for a funeral in a dark suit, sans earrings, and with beard trimmed, looked at the man expressing his condolences.

"Thanks Tommy. I'll miss him. But what have you being doing with yourself? Are you still on your fiddles?"

"I'm hardly likely to answer that with you in the force," replied Tommy Brown.

"I hear that you have a couple of kids now."

"Aye, Jimmie is three, and Davie is just a baby."

"When did you get married?"

"Christ, I'm not married. The boys have the same mother, but she didn't want them, so I'm looking after them. Anyway I must go now as I have to get to the social to sign on. It's hard work this skiving."

Billy looked around the lounge of The MacDougalls Hotel. The room was full of mourners, celebrating the life of Tom Saunders.

"I'm also leaving. I'm afraid that hanging around just brings back sad memories. But I wonder if you could do something for me? Could you keep an eye on Dad's house for about a month? I'll be back then to settle his things."

"No problems," said Tommy Brown, taking the large bunch of keys from Billy.

CHAPTER SIX

London, June 1963

"Morning Billy, how did things go at home?"

Billy Saunders looked at Fred Goodall. "Dad passed away shortly after I arrived home. It was peaceful. In a way I think he was grateful at the end. He had been in distress for some time."

"I'm sorry to hear that. I am sure, however, that you just want to get on with things. I've got the report on the drug factory raid that we carried out four days ago."

"Successful?"

"To a degree. We arrested six people and closed down the factory. Gibson was not there. I doubt if he got wind of our intentions, we were just unlucky that he wasn't there on that particular day. I have here the report from the Kent force. Check it to make sure you are happy with it."

"I'll check it later on boss if you don't mind. I want to catch up on the Brixton robbery. Bloody nuisance though, letting Gibson slip through the net after all our efforts."

"We'll get him eventually. It's just a matter of time."

Billy nodded in agreement. Scotland Yard had known for some time that Roy Gibson was the main dealer of LSD and amphetamines throughout the south of England. Gibson appeared to have a sixth sense when police action was planned against him. This had been the third time that he had escaped the net.

It was four hours later before Billy had the chance to read the report from the Kent Police. D.C. Ted Williams confirmed in the report that all those involved in the drug dealing in Kent had been arrested.

Billy placed the report in the out tray. His part of the job was finished. It was up to the Kent force and the prosecution to determine sentence.

CHAPTER SEVEN

Chatham, June 1963

Detective Sergeant Tim Jamieson wiped the rain from his face. He had been at the crime scene for an hour. A cloudburst had drenched him to the skin, despite the protection from the trees surrounding him.

"You've spoken to this Roy Smithson, the bloke who found the body?"

"Yes boss. He was walking his dog at the time. It's a regular early morning habit of his."

"It's probably a bit early to start knocking on doors, but the sooner we find out who he is the better."

Detective Constable Ted Williams looked at the body of the man sprawled at the foot of a tree.

"We've already had a telephone call at the station. Some woman complaining her old man did not return home last night. She had already checked the hospitals. Judging by the description she gave of her husband this could be him."

"A single stab wound to the heart. The victim must have known his assailant to allow him to get that close," muttered Ted Williams.

"I'm making my way back to the station now Ted; you hold on here and keep the press at bay."

Two hours later a formal identification was made of the body. Reginald Allder, a thirty six year old work study officer employed by Box Cartons at their Gillingham plant was a married man with no children. As part of the routine investigation into Mr Allder's background a check was made of his finances. Mrs Allder was astonished to hear that her husband had fifteen thousand pounds in a building society account.

"Which takes some explaining on a salary of two

thousand pounds a year," commented Detective Sergeant Jamieson. "I wonder what Mr. Allder has been up to, and who he has upset."

CHAPTER EIGHT

Chatham, June 1963

Twenty two year old builder Jack Watson came out of Chatham Town Hall after an evening of dancing. Clinging to his arm was his girl-friend Chrissie Ash, who was two months older than Jack. Chrissie, who worked as a typist in a solicitor's office in Rainham, was a quiet sort of girl. It had come as a great relief to her parents when she said she was courting.

Jack huddled close to her. There was an out of season chill in the air. They had a fifteen minute walk to Gillingham, where Chrissie lived with her parents.

The couple had been courting for six months and were at that stage in a relationship where they felt comfortable with each other. There had been no talk of a permanent relationship. They were both young. They had plenty of time before making a commitment.

Groups of squaddies and naval ratings were disgorging from the NAAFI Club as Jack and Chrissie passed. It was midnight, and the pubs and clubs of Chatham had emptied. A dark blue Royal Navy Shore Patrol vehicle stopped alongside a grey land-rover with the words Military Police emblazoned across the side.

But it was not the military police vehicles that was attracting the attention of the late night revellers, it was the civilian police car parked just outside the entrance to the NAAFI Club.

Jack and Chrissie watched as uniformed policemen bundled two men into the back of the police car. The two men were handcuffed together.

To cheers from the drunken squaddies, the police car sped away.

The fight between the army and navy personnel broke out at the precise moment the military police had expected. The squaddies were just about to enter Brompton Barracks when the verbal abuse started from the naval ratings. A running battle ensued.

Jack drew Chrissie closer to him. Another two minutes, and she would be safely indoors.

CHAPTER NINE

Chatham, July 1963

The Fountain Inn was packed. It was a Saturday night, and whilst the decent and respectable young men and women of Chatham were jiving away in the NAAFI Club, the Pavilion Dance Room, or the Paget Hall, the soldiers, sailors, and professional girls were in the Fountain Inn where a good time was guaranteed. Provided the idea of a good time consisted of getting drunk, fighting, and paying for affection.

The decor in the Fountain left a great deal to be desired. Cigarette butts littered the wooden floor. The solitary barman had already given up hope of clearing the tables. The ambiance was in keeping with the clientele.

Charlie Fox, twenty three years of age and five foot two inches in height, was sitting in a corner of the bar listening to the juke-box. Charlie had finished his bricklaying apprenticeship that week and wanted to be his own boss. There was plenty of work around. There was talk of new housing developments in nearby Rainham and Dargets Wood.

He listened attentively to the voice of Johnny Cash, oblivious to the activity around him. With the small van he had just purchased, and Johnny Cash music, he had all he wanted in life. Girls didn't interest Charlie. He had been turned down too often by them to consider taking them seriously.

He looked at his watch. It was only eight o'clock. Half the customers in the pub were already stoned out of their minds.

Charlie had noticed the tall man enter the pub earlier. The man had been standing at the bar for twenty minutes. Like Charlie, he was impervious to what was going on around him.

Charlie picked up his pint. He had seen the tall stranger before, but for the life of him he just could not think where.

The man at the bar took a sip from his glass. He placed the glass on the bar counter, and walked across to the toilet. Two minutes later he emerged from the toilet and walked out of the pub.

The glass of beer the man had been drinking was still on the bar. The glass was two thirds full.

There was no sign of the barman as Charlie picked up the stranger's glass, and wandered back to his table. There was at least a shillings worth of beer in the glass. Charlie saw no point in wasting anything.

A shout, from a soldier wearing the uniform of the Devon and Dorset Regiment, broke through the noise of the public bar. The bar went quiet. Johnny Cash was the only voice to be heard.

A shout of "Murder" has that effect.

"We'd better get the hell out of here," the squaddie yelled, "there's a body in the gents."

The public house emptied as servicemen fought to get out. They had no wish for civilian police involvement. They would have enough trouble with the military police later on.

The business girls slowly trooped out the door. It was too early in the evening for their involvement with the police. They still had a few shillings to earn.

Charlie Fox sat in an empty bar. Even the barman had disappeared. Charlie had two more Johnny Cash records to listen to. There was no way he was leaving the Fountain Inn before he had heard them.

The police entered The Fountain Inn one minute after the last working girl had vacated it. A brawl, between groups of Scottish and Irish labourers, relaxing after a hard week working on the oil refinery at Grain, had drawn a large contingent of police to the town centre. Seeing the mass exit from the Fountain Inn had aroused the curiosity of the constabulary.

An ambulance arrived two minutes after being

summoned by the police. Charlie Fox looked at the barman on the stretcher. The barman was alive, but he had clearly been the victim of a savage attack.

Charlie walked behind the bar.

In the absence of any bar staff he refilled his pint. With a bit of luck the owner would not hear about the problem at the pub until Charlie was well and truly drunk.

He closed the bolt on the inside of the pub door and resumed his seat.

Johnny Cash blared out to an attentive audience of one.

CHAPTER TEN

Chatham, March 1964

"There's no need to raise your voice. I'm trying to explain what happened to the money."

"All right Willie, calm down. I asked a perfectly reasonable question."

Willie Tosh looked at the manager of the Army and Navy public house. Willie could not argue that the question was perfectly reasonable. He had no problem with the question. It was the answer that was giving him difficulty. When he had offered his services as treasurer of the tontine club, collecting the money paid in weekly by the pub customers for their annual beano to Margate at Easter, he had thought that Easter was in late April. It came as quite a shock when the manager advised him that the holiday week-end was only a week away, and the money was required immediately.

Willie was having trouble explaining why the money was not readily available.

"For the third time of asking, where is the money?"

"Don't worry. I know exactly where it is," replied Willie.

"Well I want it by tomorrow. I have to pay for the coach."

"I'll be in tomorrow with the money. Stop panicking."

Willie breathed a deep sigh as the bar manager walked away. Willie knew exactly where the money was. He had spent every penny of the one hundred and eighty five pounds behind the bar of the very pub he was standing in. Not once had the manager queried where all the money was coming from. Willie just hoped that Charlie Fox would sub him some of the money due on the building work he was doing for him.

Willie was philosophical. If Charlie did not sub him the

money he would just start using the pubs in nearby Rochester. It would all sort itself out in the end.

CHAPTER ELEVEN

Chatham, April 1964

Jack Watson's six foot by six foot attic room was furnished with just a single bed and a bedside table. A dark suit hung from a wire hanger suspended on the back of the door. An open suitcase on the floor revealed Jack's worldly goods. A bare bulb hung from the ceiling. A small skylight, covered in grime, provided the only natural light entering the room.

Through the skylight Jack could see rain beating down. It was the first rain for several weeks. The Medway towns had been experiencing an early summer.

He could hear sounds of life in the small flat located above a newsagent in Rainham High Street. His landlady Mrs Reilly was on the move.

Jack picked up his Timex watch. He and Chrissie had bought identical "his and her" watches the previous Christmas. He glanced at the watch face and was startled to see that he had only twenty minutes to get to the dockyard. His normally good natured foreman Tom Briers had been in a foul mood the previous day, and had made it clear to Jack and the other builders that anyone late on site would be dismissed.

The smell of rancid bacon wafted through the flat. Mrs Reilly meant well, but her concept of hygiene left a great deal to be desired. The thought of eating a breakfast cooked by her turned Jack's stomach.

Keeping his head down as he descended the narrow staircase, Jack yelled to Mrs Reilly that he would see her later that evening. He usually picked up the Daily Express for Tom Briers from the newsagent but in view of Tom's comments on time-keeping he decided to give the newsagent a miss. No doubt Mr Shaw, who was not only the newsagent but also the landlord of the flat that Jack shared with Mrs Reilly, would ask Jack yet again to remind her that the rent was overdue. Jack paid his share of the rent direct to Mrs Reilly every Friday, and on each occasion had received her assurance that she would pay the rent to the landlord. It had come as a shock to Jack when Mr Shaw advised him the previous week that the rent had not been paid for two months. Jack wondered how long his patience would last.

The Maidstone & District dockyard bound bus was packed, as dockyard mateys made their way to the town's main employer. With over six thousand people working there the dockyard was the life and soul of Chatham.

Traffic was unusually slow that morning due to the heavy downpour. Good fortune was on Jack's side however, as Tom Briers was also delayed due to the weather, arriving on site ten minutes after Jack.

But Jack had other things on his mind. When he and Chrissie had left the Royal Cinema at Rainham the previous evening she had told him that she was pregnant. It must have been watching Elvis in "Love me Tender" that gave her the courage to tell Jack. She had been dropping hints lately about settling down, but Jack was not sure if he was ready for that sort of commitment.

Ten hours after arriving at the building site, Tom Briers called a halt to the day's activities. Despite the rain a great deal of progress had been made on the trench for the new drainage system being installed at the dockyard. "Put the tools away, make sure you are not late in the morning, and don't forget my bloody newspaper tomorrow," was the foreman's parting comment, throwing Jack the key to the storage hut.

Jack threw his spade to the ground and considered his problems. He would almost certainly be homeless by the end of the week if Mrs Reilly did not come up with the rent that she owed, and Chrissie's father would probably kill him when he discovered that his daughter was pregnant.

"Which" he reflected, "would at least solve the rent problem".

"Penny for them."

Jack looked up to find Chrissie gazing at him.

"We have to talk."

Jack nodded. When she had told him that she was pregnant he had been at a loss for words. "Not now, can I see you this evening? Eight o'clock at the cafe down the Strand."

"I'll be there," she replied.

Jack watched as she headed towards the bus stop on Military Road. With a deep sigh he wandered across to the storage hut.

Chrissie, deep in thought, looked up briefly as she saw the sailor and two civilians approach. Lowering her head again she failed to see the smile on the face of the tallest man as he looked at her.

She was at the bus-stop before she remembered where she had seen two of the passers-by before. The previous summer, handcuffed together, getting into a police car at the NAAFI Club.

***

Jack completed the task of placing all the tools in the hut and fumbled in his pocket for the padlock key. He hoped that Mrs Reilly would boil some water for him on her cooker. He needed a good scrub before meeting Chrissie. It was a nuisance not having a bathroom in the flat, although the lack of bathing facilities did not seem to bother Mrs Reilly.

Jack froze. He heard voices outside the hut. Voices raised in anger. He heard the words "drugs", "onto you", and "police". He stepped closer to the door of the hut, which was slightly ajar.

The spade that Jack had just placed against a large toolbox fell to the ground. The conversation outside the hut abruptly ceased. The door to the hut flew open.

Jack was no fool. He had been aware from his early teens that drugs could kill. He just did not realise that a knife could form part of the killing process. He never felt the thin blade pierce his heart. Nor did he feel Donnie Grey push him into the muddy trench, nor feel the mud as it covered his body.

***

At nine o'clock that evening Chrissie Ash reached the conclusion that Jack was not going to turn up for their date. She went home and waited for him to contact her. She had seen how troubled he had been, when she had told him that she was pregnant. She had seen his reaction, when she had raised the question of settling down.

It took three days for her to pluck up enough courage to visit Jack's flat. There was no reply to her repeated knocking on the door of the flat.

On enquiring at the newsagent, she was informed that Mrs Reilly had been evicted. The newsagent stated that he had no idea where Jack was, but thought it strange that he had not even bothered to collect his few possessions.

CHAPTER TWELVE

Chatham, April 1964

It was Andy Spiers' girl friend who prompted him to make the move away from the Medway towns. Ann Stanton maintained that she was having trouble getting a proper job because of her prison record. Andy refrained from pointing out that, apart from prostitution, she had not worked since leaving school eight years earlier.

But Andy did not need much persuading when the subject of moving arose. He was also restless. He had been in the same job since leaving school. He had long since stopped communicating with his parents, and the police were taking an unhealthy interest in him. There was nothing to hold him in the Medway towns.

Donnie Grey listened attentively to Andy. It was ten o'clock on a Sunday morning, too early for the pubs to open, but the Eleven Stops Coffee Shop in Rochester High Street did a mean breakfast. Not that bacon and eggs was the reason for the visit. When Donnie had run into Andy the previous evening in the Eagle pub Andy had stressed the importance of an early meeting.

"I wake up every morning expecting the police to be hammering on the door. We are pushing our luck Donnie. If they ever find out what we have done, we'll be in prison for a long time. I'm leaving."

"Agreed, any idea where you'll go?"

"No. I'll speak to Ann about it. We won't go too far away. Perhaps London, so we can visit Chatham whenever we want."

"Well, there's no point in me hanging about either."

The following day Andy Spiers and Ann Stanton left the Medway towns. Donnie Grey waited a further day before making his departure.

CHAPTER THIRTEEN

Chatham, April 1964

Ted Ashcroft, sitting in the office of the Admiralty Police in Chatham Dockyard, answered the telephone at the first ring. He listened carefully to what was being said.

"I'll come right over."

Five minutes later he was in the office of the Naval Police.

"Hello Ted, how long has it been, four years?"

Ted Ashcroft looked at the new officer in charge of the Naval Police. He had last seen Lt. Roy Evans at Portsmouth Dockyard, when they worked together on an arson attack on one of the ships. Due to their combined efforts the arsonist was arrested.

"So, Petty Officer Piper has done a runner has he?"

"That would appear to be the case. He was due to report for duty three days ago following a forty eight hour pass. His absence was initially reported to his ship's police. It took a few days for the news to filter down to me although in fairness to the ship's crew no one knew that Piper was under surveillance."

"Has he taken anything with him?"

"It's difficult to tell. We've checked his quarters. For all we know he could have packed a suitcase with civilian clothes."

"I'll submit a "Missing Person" report to the Chatham Police. I think we can safely assume however that he has deserted."

CHAPTER FOURTEEN

Chatham, November 1964

"He's taken a terrible beating, particularly the blow to the head. It looks like the work of a maniac."

Detective Inspector John Savage looked around the murder scene. At eleven o'clock on a Sunday morning Luton Recreation Ground, a sports area that would normally have been crowded with Sunday League footballers, was virtually deserted. John Savage accompanied by two other investigating officers, three uniformed police officers, and a two man forensic team, were the only signs of life.

"It could be the work of two people, judging by the beating he has taken. He's not exactly on the small side. Have we any idea who he is?"

"D.C. Williams is making enquiries as we speak," replied Detective Sergeant Bill Ambrose.

"When Williams gets back to the station get him to report to me straight away. I have to be at a christening in an hour. The wife will murder me if I'm late."

"OK John. I'll tell the coroner's people to take the body away. There's not much we can do here now. The crime scene is far enough away from the football pitches not to be a problem. I'll tell the uniformed boys to admit the footballers before they start a riot."

***

Later that day Ted Williams submitted his formal report to John Savage. The report stated that the victim was a thirty eight year old supermarket check-out operator who lived in the area of the playing fields. James Lewis had spent most of the previous evening in the Luton Tavern public house. He had left the pub at ten thirty. His wife had assumed that he had gone to a friend's house for an all night card school, a frequent habit of his. He normally walked through the playing fields on his way home from the public house. Mrs Lewis had stated that her husband had no enemies. He was a normal family man who liked to have a drink and play darts. Members of the pub darts and domino teams were being interviewed to see if they could shed any light on his murder. Mrs Lewis and her twin ten year old sons were staying with her mother in Rainham should the police wish to question her again.

CHAPTER FIFTEEN

Inverness, April 1965

Donnie Grey shivered. He was beginning to wonder if he would ever feel warm again. The warmth of the previous Summer had long been forgotten, overtaken by a Winter more fierce than Donnie had ever experienced. The arrival of Spring had brought some relief. The irony was that Donnie was now settled. At the age of twenty five he had found contentment in life that he had never experienced before.

The screams of children rolling eggs down the small hillock at Inverness Castle awoke Donnie from his day-dreaming. It was Easter, and the building trade had shut down for a long week-end.

Donnie turned to the couple sitting beside him on the grass.

"I'm going back to the pub to get packed. I'll be moving in with Sheila Jennison first thing tomorrow, but I'll be around this evening to baby-sit."

Ian Collins nodded. His wife Shona smiled. Baby Susan gurgled.

Donnie Grey strolled down the castle hill with a smile on his face. Life was good.

***

Twelve months earlier Donnie had stood at London's Kings Cross Station. He had checked the train indicator board. Geography was not his strong point, but if he was correct, Inverness was about as far away as he could get from London by train.

Ten hours and five hundred miles later, Donnie found himself standing in the public bar of the Academy Inn, one hundred yards from Inverness railway station. His first impression was not favourable. But he was tired, and the rail network had ground to a halt for the day. Like it or not, Donnie Grey was stuck in Inverness for at least one night.

He had gone into the station buffet the moment he got off the train. His enquiry as to where he could get a bed for the night brought a grunt from a counter assistant who had only one thought in mind – closing.

His second stop, at the Garry Bar fifty yards from the station, resulted in verbal abuse from two of the customers. Asking for a pint of mild beer was Donnie's first mistake. Asking for a pint glass with a handle was the second. When the drunken customers realised that Donnie was English, the abuse started.

Donnie left the bar, but got the message. Not only were the English not welcome, but the only beer on sale was "light or heavy".

It was in the Merkinch Arms that good luck turned Donnie's way. Bracing himself for further abuse, he asked the attractive barmaid for "a pint of heavy."

Donnie looked at the beer which had been placed in front of him.

"It's safe to drink, I promise you" said the barmaid, with a twinkle in her eye.

Donnie picked up the glass.

The barmaid looked at the suitcase that Donnie had placed on the floor. "Just off the London train?"

Donnie nodded. "Yes, I need a place to bed down to-night, and I'll be straight back on it tomorrow."

"We do bed and breakfast here. I'll check with the manager to see if there are any vacancies."

That night Donnie Grey had the dream for the first time. A dream of a white hand reaching out of the darkness. He awoke in a panic.

It was several hours before he closed his eyes again.

***

Reaching the foot of the castle hill, Donnie broke into a smile. The one night had turned into a year. He had stayed at the Merkinch Arms during this time. He had found employment as a labourer working on the construction of a new housing estate. It had taken him a few weeks to establish a rapport with the regulars of the public house. It had taken the charm of Shona Collins, the friendly barmaid on the night of his arrival, to break the ice between the dour locals and the quiet Englishman. Three months after his first encounter with Shona, he was introduced to her bank clerk husband Ian, and their daughter Susan. It was six months before Shona mentioned that she had lived in Chatham as a child. Her father had been an officer in the Royal Engineers, stationed at Brompton Barracks. He had died five years earlier, but she still had a brother serving in the army at Aldershot.

That evening Donnie relaxed in the Collins living room of their small flat. He enjoyed baby-sitting. He felt depressed when he thought of his sister. But being with baby Susan made him feel better.

CHAPTER SIXTEEN

Inverness, July 1965

Sheila Jennison placed the meal in front of Donnie Grey, and took her place at the table. Donnie had been living with her for three months and Sheila was content. Not only was Donnie the perfect lover, he was kind and considerate to her. He had his moments, moments stretching to days, when he did not speak to her, but that suited her. She was not one for lengthy conversations.

"Is your meal all right?"

Donnie awoke from his day-dreaming. "What? Oh, yes its fine thanks."

"What's bothering you, Donnie?"

Donnie stood up. "For God's sake woman will you stop asking so many bloody questions."

Sheila rose from the table. "I don't need this Donnie, and I certainly don't deserve it."

Donnie looked at Sheila. How could he tell her that he was sick to death of being smothered by her? He now regretted taking up the offer she had made when she had overheard him remark to one of the other staff in the Harbour Inn, that he wanted to live in a homely environment. At the time the bed and breakfast arrangement at the Merkinch Arms had ceased to be appealing.

When they had ended up in bed together, two weeks after he had moved into her house, it was wonderful. The sex was still good, but Sheila was so possessive.

"I'm sorry Sheila; I have a lot on my mind."

But Donnie knew that he was just putting off the inevitable. At some point he had to tell her that he was moving out.

CHAPTER SEVENTEEN

Inverness, August 1965

Tommy Brown, after eleven years of practice since leaving high school, could have qualified for a degree in idleness. He had successfully reached the age of twenty six without ever having held a job. Tommy would no doubt have taken exception to anyone making this observation, pointing out that making a living by defrauding the unemployment benefits office, and operating other scams, was hard work.

Tommy yawned, stretched his legs, and scratched himself. The sun was streaming through the bedroom window of his two bedroom house situated in the heart of the Ferry council estate. He looked at the Donald Duck alarm clock on his bedside cabinet. It was nine o'clock, which meant that he had two hours to get down to the town centre. A visit to the town centre was necessary. He had an appointment at the bank. Today was the start of the rest of his life, a different life, a life of employment.

Tommy's metamorphosis had begun the previous week, when he was approached by Peter Salah, a Polish exile who had settled in Inverness after the Second World War, with the proposition that he and Tommy purchase a small van and go into the light removals business. Tommy had actually been considering acquiring a vehicle for use in removals, although he had burglary in mind rather than the legitimate removal of household effects. But when Tommy considered the two young sons he was bringing up, he saw merit in Peter Salah's proposition. Hence the unusual step of Tommy Brown planning to go into a bank by the front door.

Tommy clambered out of bed and looked out of the bedroom window. In the garden next door he could see his neighbour Sheila Jennison in her nightdress, hanging out her washing. Tommy watched her for a few moments. She was a tasty bit of stuff. He hastily drew back from the window as, having completed her task, Sheila turned to re-enter her house.

Tommy was woken out of his daydreaming by a yell from his son Jimmie, informing him that Davie had wet the bed, a bed he shared with Jimmie.

For a brief moment Tommy thought of dumping the boys with their mother.

***

In the adjoining house Sheila Jennison was making an observation to Donnie Grey.

"That dirty sod next door was looking at me again. He's always peering out that window hoping to catch me in my underwear. I've a good mind to report him to the unemployment benefit office. The pervert must be on some sort of fiddle. He never does any work, but he's always in the pub."

Donnie Grey looked at her. Donnie was depressed. "Sod it, I'm off to the pub," he said.

"But the pub doesn't open for two hours. I thought you had taken the day off so we could go out together."

Donnie slammed the front door behind him as he left the house.

CHAPTER EIGHTEEN

Inverness, December 1966

Despite Donnie Grey's determination to leave Sheila Jennison he was still with her twenty months after he had moved in. Their relationship only survived because she was either working in the Harbour Inn or, when she was at home, Donnie was out drinking.

In a rare moment of weakness, Donnie decided to visit the Harbour Inn when Sheila was working there. The pub was busy with the crews from two Scandinavian freighters jostling with the Ferry locals.

A contretemps arose when Sheila took exception to a comment passed by Stewart MacInver after serving him a round of drinks. Rumour had it that MacInver had fled London after killing a man in a pub for knocking his drink over.

"There's no need for language like that to the lady," Donnie Grey said to a stunned MacInver.

"Lady! That cow is no lady, you silly sod."

Donnie Grey hit MacInver full in the face. MacInver fell to the ground.

MacInver picked himself off the floor. "You're dead you bastard, you're dead." Standing upright, MacInver took a swing at Donnie, just as Sheila stepped in between the men. Sheila took the full blow. She fell to the ground.

It took four seamen to hold back MacInver.

MacInver's parting words, as he was escorted from the public house by three policemen, were – "You're a walking dead man. We'll meet again."

Two days later two officers from the Metropolitan Police arrived in Inverness to escort MacInver back to London to face a murder charge.

Sheila was off work for three months with a broken jaw. During this time Donnie did not have the heart to tell her that he was leaving.

***

On Christmas Eve Donnie paid the Collins family a visit. Shona was pleased to see him. Baby Susan was now twenty months old. She reminded Donnie of his sister at that age.

Donnie spent the remainder of Christmas Eve on his own in the Ness Bar.

The barmaid got quite concerned at one point. She was sure that the big man sitting on his own was crying.

CHAPTER NINETEEN

Inverness, April 1967

Clutching the machete in his right hand, five year old Davie Brown peered round the broken fence at the rear of the house he shared with his father Tommy and elder brother Jimmie. There was no woman in the household. Davie had never known the love of a mother. He had arrived in the world as the result of a brief but passionate encounter between his father and a woman behind the grandstand at the local Clachnacuddin football ground, whilst the home team were involved in a cup game against local rivals Thistle. It is fair to say that Tommy scored more than Thistle did that day. Davie had got quite used to not having a mother around the house. He had been told by one of the older kids in the neighbourhood that his mother was Irene Norman, who lived on her own in a small house, half a mile from Davie's home. Davie had only ever seen her on four occasions, and on each occasion she had completely ignored him. He had never received birthday or Christmas presents from her. Davie didn't mind. He couldn't stand the woman.

He had seen the ginger cat earlier. The cat had run away every time Davie had approached. Living in the Ferry area the cat had probably already used up eight of its nine lives, but the evil look in Davie's eye had Mrs Ellis's old moggy seriously worried.

Holding his breath, Davie waited patiently. He peered round the fence again. He could see the cat approaching. He stepped back, and counted. One, two, four. Maths was not Davie's strong point in his first year at infant school.

Stepping from behind the fence, Davie lifted his arm. The machete left his hand with the firm intent of decapitating the love of Mrs Ellis's life.

So intent was Davie on his mission that he failed to hear the creak of the back gate opening in the adjoining garden. Nor did he see Donnie Grey tread onto the path that ran at the rear of the terraced houses. He did not even see Donnie kneel down to stroke the cat. In fact he saw nothing of Donnie at all. But he heard him.

The pain of a machete slicing across the face would have brought a scream from anyone.

Davie took a tentative step towards Donnie Grey. Donnie Grey was kneeling on the ground, blood streaming from his face. Davie stared in horror.

"You little bastard" screamed Donnie, getting to his feet, "I'll bloody murder you."

Davie had only taken one step before Donnie's hand caught him across the head. Davie fell to the ground, picked himself up, and ran. He knew that the man lived with the woman next door. The other kids reckoned that the woman was "mad, and a tart." He had no idea what "a tart" was, but he knew what "mad" meant, and he saw all the signs of it on the bloody face of the man he had just injured. He had never met the man before. But Davie wasn't going to hang about to make formal introductions.

Twenty minutes later Donnie Grey was in casualty. The cut ran from his hairline to his jaw, just missing his eye. It took two hours of painful stitching before Donnie was allowed to leave the hospital. When asked what had caused the laceration Donnie abruptly stated that he had an accident whilst chopping firewood. There was no way that he was going to admit that a five year old child had caused the injury.

Davie Brown did not mention the incident to his family.

CHAPTER TWENTY

Chatham, April 1967

Detective Inspector Graham Simpson looked closely at the body. He could see the extensive bruising to the face. He had a feeling that the bruising extended to the rest of the body. He would know for sure once the pathologist had undressed the body back at the police morgue.

"He's been dead about an hour by all accounts. What do you reckon he was doing out here?"

"Your guess is as good as mine boss."

Graham Simpson looked around the playing field behind Gillingham council offices. The area had already been sealed off by the police. The noise of children had faded. The creak of a swing, caught by the wind, broke the silence.

"This is the second middle aged man in three years murdered in the area of a playing field. It's probably a coincidence, but let's find out exactly who Mr Lawson was, and what he was doing in a children's play area."

Detective Constable Ted Williams stared at the body. "He's had a right going over, that's for sure. Okay to take him away?"

Graham Simpson nodded to the police undertaker.

"Well let's carry on with the investigation. You can do the leg-work Williams; it'll be good experience for you. Check the local shops and public houses to see if anyone knows who he is."

Ted Williams looked at his inspector.

"Okay boss. I'll keep you informed."

***

It took twenty four hours before it was confirmed that the

dead man was Andrew Lawson, a thirty nine year old civil servant employed by Gillingham Council. Staff at the Prince Albert public house confirmed that Mr Wilson had been in the bar early in the evening, two hours before the body was discovered. His wife and ten year old son arrived back from an overnight stay with in-laws in Sevenoaks to be greeted with the news of his murder.

CHAPTER TWENTY ONE

Inverness, June 1967

Sheila Jennison had never had much sustained genuine affection in her life. Her quiet temperament, often seen as moody, quickly became a turn-off for any man initially attracted by her looks. Sheila was not promiscuous, but having been seen with a number of boy-friends her neighbours had formed the conclusion that she was free and easy with her affections. Nothing could have been further from the truth. Which explains why, despite Donnie Grey's disfigurement, and their frequent disagreements, she was reluctant to let Donnie go. During the three months she was recovering from her jaw injury, Donnie had attended to all her needs. The inevitable happened. For the first time in her life, at the age of twenty six, Sheila Jennison found herself in love.

Donnie was expecting some sort of reaction from her when he told her that he was leaving, but he was taken aback by the scale of it.

"Don't leave me Donnie. You're the only good thing that's ever happened to me. Men have treated me like dirt all my life."

"I'm sorry Sheila but I think it would be better if we parted. We hardly speak to each other. You're moody all the time. I need a life."

Donnie put his arm around her.

Sheila pulled herself away from him. "I'm not good enough for you, am I? You're just like all the rest of them. You all think I'm odd. I've seen the way you all look at me."

"Come on Sheila, love."

"Love? You don't know the meaning of the word. I know what love means. It means working in a stinking bar every night being leered at by drunken men, just so that you can have enough money to provide a decent home for the man you love. I've loved you from the moment I saw you. I even find your scar attractive. I'll never stop loving you. I know there is a dark side to you Donnie, I've seen it surface. Jekyll and Hyde, that's who you are." Donnie took all the abuse that was thrown at him. It was a testament to the affection he had for Sheila. The murderous side of Donnie remained hidden.

"I'm sorry, Sheila."

"Sorry, I'll give you sorry."

Donnie's timing for giving out bad news was abysmal. It was one o'clock in the morning. After a hectic evening at the Harbour Inn, tending to the needs of drunken and pawing merchant seamen, Sheila had come home to the man she loved. She was snuggling up to him in bed when he broke the news.

The neighbourhood awoke to the sound of screaming. A frying pan crashed through the kitchen window, followed by a set of saucepans.

Tommy Brown awoke to the sound of "I've given you all my love."

Wide awake by now, Tommy looked around his room. He was fairly certain that he had gone to bed on his own but it had been a heavy night in the Harbour Inn.

He heard the voice again. He looked out of his window. Lights were coming on in nearby houses. Regardless of the time, day or night, nobody in the district ever missed a good fight, and this one sounded promising.

In the dim glow of a street light he could see Donnie Grey, suitcase in hand, walking down the pathway of Sheila Jennison's house. Sheila, oblivious to the fact that she was wearing only a baby-doll nightie, stood in the doorway with tears streaming down her face.

"Don't leave me, Donnie", she wailed.

Donnie was dejected. He had no idea that Sheila had felt so strongly about him. But there was no going back. Half an hour after leaving her he booked into a small bed and breakfast establishment in the town centre. He was determined to make himself comfortable, whilst he decided on his next move.

But that spiteful mistress, Fate, had other plans for Donnie.

Two days after being ejected from the home he had shared with Sheila Jennison, Donnie Grey found himself in new surroundings. They were not as luxurious as his temporary bed and breakfast accommodation, but police cells are not renowned for comfort.

Donnie had been in several bars that evening before he ended up in the Garry Bar. He was depressed. For three years he had successfully blocked his mind to the events in Chatham that had precipitated his move to Inverness. He was also depressed about his sister and he had lately been thinking rather a lot about Shona Collins.

Donnie looked up. The elderly man sitting at the other end of the bar averted his gaze as Donnie looked at him.

"What are you looking at you old git? Never seen a scar before?"

Without giving the man a chance to respond, Donnie strode across the room. Donnie lost complete control.

A week later he was sentenced to two years imprisonment for assault.

Sheila Jennison was in the courtroom as Donnie was sentenced.

"I'll wait for you," she shouted, as he was taken away.

CHAPTER TWENTY TWO

London, January 1969

Donnie Grey was three months into his prison sentence, sharing a two man cell with a small time forger and a career burglar, when the decision was made that he should be transferred to another prison. Inverness Prison was experiencing over-crowding. In order to ease the congestion a number of prisoners were to be dispersed throughout the country. On hearing the news that there was the possibility of a transfer, Donnie requested a move closer to his home town of Chatham. Donnie had Maidstone Prison in mind when he put his name forward for consideration.

Perhaps Maidstone Prison was also experiencing over-crowding. More likely Donnie's request for a transfer fell into the hands of one of the more sadistic officers who controlled the lives of the prisoners. Whatever the reason behind the decision, one month after submitting his transfer request, Donnie Grey found himself in the most notorious prison in England, London's Wormwood Scrubs.

Donnie proved to be a model prisoner and earned himself early release after eighteen months. Being a model prisoner came easy to him as he spent most of his sentence being treated in the prison hospital. But Donnie had overlooked one thing in making his transfer request from Inverness Prison to a south of England prison – Stewart MacInver.

The realisation that MacInver was also a prisoner in the Scrubs, hit Donnie on day three of his internment, when his face was pushed into his slopping out bucket.

"Well, fancy meeting you in here. I said we'd meet again didn't I? Although I didn't think you'd save me the journey to Inverness. Two years I've been in this hole. Every day of those two years I've looked forward to the day I ran into you again. Suddenly my whole life feels better. Mind you, by the look of your ugly face it looks as though someone has beaten me to it."

His face covered in excrement, Donnie Grey looked into the hateful face of Stewart MacInver.

For the next fifteen months Donnie Grey lived in fear. His only solace was in the prison hospital, where he was treated for physical injuries and mental distress. Each night of those fifteen months Donnie awoke in a cold sweat. Recurring nightmares tormented him: A bloody knife: A white hand emerging from a dark abyss: A young girl crying. The physical pain was kept away by morphine, the mental torment by hallucinatory inducing drugs. Donnie Grey's mind floated between tranquillity and insanity.

In Inverness Prison Donnie had rubbed shoulders with thieves and fraudsters. He even recalled, with some affection, his two cell mates, the smooth talking forger and the innocuous burglar. In Wormwood Scrubs he was mixing with the scum of the earth.

The day prior to Donnie's release from prison he was visited in his two man cell by MacInver. Donnie's cell mate, a child killer from Hull, beat a hasty retreat when he saw MacInver in the cell doorway.

"Just to let you know that I'm not finished with you. I'll be out one day, and I'll track you down," was MacInver's parting words to Donnie.

Donnie Grey came out of prison a broken man.

He left behind the pile of unopened letters.

The following day the prison officials returned the bundle of letters to Sheila Jennison.

CHAPTER TWENTY THREE

London, December 1970

Donnie Grey turned on the second bar of the small electric fire. He shivered. London seemed reluctant to shake off a winter that had begun with a flurry of snow in the first week of November, and had continued unabated since then.

He had settled back into a life of freedom quite easily. With the assistance of a prisoners' aid charity he had found a small bedsit just off Kilburn High Street in north London. A visit to one of the many Irish pubs in the area had quickly found him work with a firm of building contractors in central London.

He still had nightmares, but he was getting back to normal.

Big Ben rang out midnight.

Donnie stared at the small black and white television. He sat entranced as Andy Stewart, hosting a New Year's Eve ceilidh from Glasgow, led the other performers and audience in the singing of Auld Lang Syne. Donnie had not thought of Shona Collins for some time.

An hour later, drowned in memories, he watched the white dot disappear from the screen. It was forty minutes later before he turned the television off. As he lay in bed, staring at the ceiling, tears streamed down his face.

CHAPTER TWENTY FOUR

London, March 1971

"Fancy a drink after work? The Green Man in Cheapside does a mean pint."

Donnie Grey looked at Steve Riley, the site foreman. He had kept himself to himself since his release from prison, but the thought of a pint and a bit of company was appealing.

"Suits me Steve, I'm not exactly in a hurry to get back to a poky room and a packet of Vesta Curry."

"The pub will be packed with tottie from the offices. I've never seen so much talent in one area in my life. I think most of them welcome the company of a real man after a day with these arrogant ponces in suits."

Donnie laughed.

"I thought you were a married man?"

"With three kids, but what the wife doesn't see..."

***

"Jesus. I see what you mean about talent. The place is heaving with it."

Steve Riley drained his pint. "Sup up. It's your round next."

Donnie picked up Steve's empty glass, and walked to the bar. He had to fight his way through a group of office workers. "Two pints of best bitter please love," said Donnie to a harassed barmaid.

"Make it three pints, and a gin and tonic."

Donnie turned round.

"I thought it was you Donnie. I saw you sitting in the corner."

"Andy, what are you doing here?"

"I've been in London since I left Chatham. Must be seven years now."

"I take it that the gin and tonic is for a lady friend then?"

"Ann. You remember Ann Stanton don't you? She's in the restaurant. Why don't you join us?"

"Hardly, I'm not exactly dressed for a restaurant. Wearing builders gear I'm lucky to get served a pint."

"I take your point. But sit tight. Ann and I will have finished our meal shortly. We'll come through and join you."

"A friend of yours?" enquired Steve Riley, as Donnie placed his pint in front of him.

"Sort of," replied Donnie. "Just someone I used to know. He's coming through to the bar shortly."

Twenty minutes later the smell of perfume filled Donnie's nostrils. He looked up to see Ann Stanton smiling down at him. "Donnie, it's..." she stopped, and then continued, "what the hell have you done to your face?"

Before Donnie had a chance to reply, Ann Stanton spoke again. "Who's your friend?"

Donnie made the introductions.

"I'll leave you with Steve for a few minutes Ann, whilst Donnie and I go to the bar and catch up on the gossip."

"Don't rush. I quite like the idea of some time with Steve."

Donnie and Andy Spiers compared the events in their lives over the previous seven years – Donnie's move to Inverness, his prison spells, the people he had met in prison, and the Davie Brown incident. During Donnie's period in Inverness and in prison, Andy Spiers and Ann Stanton had returned to Chatham on several occasions.

In a state of drunkenness Donnie confided his secret to an attentive Andy Spiers; the fact that he had murdered someone. Donnie was not to know that this indiscreet confession would lead to disastrous consequences thirty years later. He had forgotten just how evil Andy Spiers was.

"Judging by what you say about the inmates, I would be well advised to stay out of the nick. Mind you Ann and I have no intentions of spending any time there. We're too clever for that."

That night Donnie had nightmares. The nightmares were not entirely due to the Vesta curry.

The following day he visited a back street pub in Kilburn. It cost him ten pounds for the sachet of white powder.

CHAPTER TWENTY FIVE

London, April 1972

Donnie Grey looked at the writing on the wall of his bedsit. He tried to make sense of the jumbled letters. He had trouble discerning what language it was, or even if it was a language. The wall and the letters moved as he stared at them. He averted his gaze, and lowered his head to the floor. He whimpered as he watched the carpet rising off the floor in undulating waves. He watched as the strange words on the wall drifted across the carpet and slowly climbed the filthy sheet covering his naked body. He screamed as an alphabet of letters entered his mouth. His mind caved in.

The drink and drugs had finally taken their toll on Donnie. A month after his encounter with Andy Spiers he had been ejected from the building site as he was considered a safety hazard to all he worked with. Steve Riley had supported him as much as he could, but when the construction project manager stated that the contract would be terminated if Donnie was not removed from site, even Steve's loyalty came to an end.

Donnie lived in a twilight world for twelve months. Most of this time he lived as a down and out in the streets of Soho, returning to his bedsit on the rare occasions when he remembered that he had a home. Despite all the efforts of the prisoners' aid society, Donnie was free-wheeling downhill fast.

Donnie's rescue came in the form of his landlord, a landlord who had been trying for three months to have him evicted. Finally, obtaining a court order for eviction, the landlord forced entry to Donnie's bedsit. This timely intervention saved Donnie's life. Thirty minutes after the enforced entry Donnie Grey was admitted to hospital.

Six weeks later he was discharged. He was free of drugs, but homeless.

CHAPTER TWENTY SIX

Inverness, March 1973

Two years in London was enough for Donnie Grey. He realised that unless he made a complete break away from the London drug scene, there was little chance of him leading a normal life. Whilst recovering in hospital, Donnie reflected on the time he had spent in Inverness with Shona Collins and her family.

Once again Donnie found himself at Kings Cross station. On this occasion however, he knew exactly where he was going. One hour after his arrival in Inverness he had moved back into his bed and breakfast accommodation in the Merkinch Arms. On enquiring about Shona Collins, he was advised that she had left the area following the death of her husband. When asked where she had moved to, the reply was "down south."

The day after his arrival Donnie reported to a construction site, hoping to find employment. His luck was in.

For the next two years Donnie kept his head down. He stayed off the drugs. But he still liked a drink.

***

Donnie was suddenly aware that someone was touching his face.

"What have you done to yourself?"

Donnie pulled back, startled.

"What have you done to yourself?" Shona Collins repeated.

Donnie shook his head. He had been in the Merkinch Arms for an hour. He was still in his work clothes. "What are you doing here Shona? I heard that you left the area five years ago, when Ian died."

"I did. I've only been back in Inverness a week. I ran into one of the pub regulars in the High Street. He said that you were back in town and lived here. I thought I'd look in on the off-chance of seeing you. When Ian died I went to live with my brother in Aldershot. When my brother was posted to Germany last month, I decided to move back to Inverness."

Donnie stared at Shona.

"Well, that's what I've been up to. How about you Donnie? You look as though you've been in the wars."

Donnie sighed.

"For a start, tell me how you got that scar on your face?"

"I'll tell you one day, I promise, but not now."

"Would you like to come up to my house to see Susan?"

Donnie stood up. "Give me half an hour. I'll have a wash and get out of these work clothes."

Ten months later Donnie and Shona were married.

He did not see Sheila Jennison standing outside the registry office. He did not see her collapse.

By the time the ambulance had arrived to tend to Sheila's needs, Donnie and Shona were on the way to their wedding reception.

CHAPTER TWENTY SEVEN

Inverness, March 1973

Whilst Donnie Grey was succeeding in bringing his life back to normality, life for Sheila Jennison was grim. Sheila's obsession with Donnie had reduced her to a state of manic depression. Receiving the batch of unopened letters from the prison authorities had been a huge blow to the little self-esteem she had left. Seeing Donnie at the registry office was the final straw.

For a period of four years the lives of Donnie Grey and Sheila Jennison had run parallel, with each of them alternating between hospital, drugs and alcohol. In Sheila's case the drugs were medication, to keep at bay the devils tormenting her.

But whilst Donnie only had himself to worry about, Sheila had a motherly role to perform. Donnie Grey's daughter was born eight months after he walked out on Sheila. Had Donnie taken the time to read any of the letters that Sheila had sent to him whilst he was in prison, he would have been aware, that he was a father.

Two hours after seeing Donnie at the registry office, Sheila Jennison was admitted to a psychiatric hospital. Her five year old daughter was taken into care.

CHAPTER TWENTY EIGHT

Rainham, October 1975

Bert Woodlands staggered out of the Railway Tavern having just been ejected by the police. The police involvement had arisen as a result of a verbal dispute earlier in the evening between Bert and a local builder, one of the pub's regular customers. The landlord had taken the side of the builder in the dispute, despite the fact that the builder had physically threatened Bert. Bert had initially calmed down after the landlord's intervention, but several drinks later he became aggressive. On being refused a further drink he threw a beer glass at the landlord.

Bert found himself out in the street, walking home to his wife and two children. He was dreading getting home. He was already two hours late for his eleven-year-old son's birthday party. He had been drinking heavily every evening since his redundancy three weeks earlier. He was lucky the police had treated him so lightly when they had picked him up the previous week.

He was halfway down the dark alleyway leading off the High Street before he realised that there was someone behind him. He stepped to one side to allow the other person to pass him, and held onto the wire fence for support. He realised he had drunk too much. It was not as though he could afford it. At the time of his redundancy it had not bothered him. As a fully qualified electrician he would find another position easily. That was the basis of the argument he had been having with the builder in the pub earlier on. The man who had said that electricians were ten a penny, and there was no work available locally.

Bert suddenly realised that he could no longer hear footsteps behind him. He turned round. Despite the poor lighting in the alleyway he recognised the man immediately.

Bert felt a pain spreading through his chest. "Christ. Not a heart attack. Not at my age surely," he muttered as he clutched his chest.

Bert felt the warm liquid on his hand. He was on the ground before he realised it was blood.

***

"How many unsolved murders do we have on the books at present?" Sergeant Ted Williams looked up at Inspector Graham Johns.

"Six including this one, but we have solved fourteen murders in the past eleven years. Our clear up rate is higher than the national average. Considering how under-manned we are, and the strong military presence in the area with the inherent problems that brings, we've done well."

"We'll have to concentrate our resources on young Sally Trebor's killing. The public get uptight when school-kids are murdered. I've got the Chief Super on my back. The press are having a field day, accusing us of incompetence. Do what you can with this one Ted."

"Okay boss. Are you going to Tom Matthews' retirement do tonight?"

"I'll be there."

"I'll see you later on then."

CHAPTER TWENTY NINE

Chatham, May 1979

At the age of sixty-nine Nora Wilkins could lay claim to the fact that she had seen every possible way in which the great British public treated public toilets. But even *she* was shocked when she stepped into the toilets at the Hempstead Valley shopping centre to be confronted with a dark fluid, streaking across the floor from the wash hand basins to one of the stalls. The shopping mall had only been in existence a matter of months and the toilet area was Nora's pride and joy.

Nora carefully avoided stepping on the sticky floor and covered her mouth as she walked to the stall. She was accustomed to nasty toilet odours, but this was something new to her.

She screamed as she realised the source of the smell. The body of a large man sat on the toilet seat. Congealed blood covered his chest.

***

"According to the contents of his wallet his name is Sydney Cooper from Pine Tree Grove, just round the corner from here. Aged thirty-six, married with a couple of kids. He worked as a bank clerk in Rainham. He had been shopping at the Savacentre. The shopping bag was by his body. That's as much as we know at the moment. He had forty pounds in his wallet so the motive was clearly not robbery. The killing must have happened shortly after the centre closed down a couple of hours ago. I should think his wife is a bit concerned at his late arrival home."

Detective Inspector Graham Simpson looked at the mutilated body.

"Would you mind informing Mrs Cooper? The sooner she knows the better."

Five minutes later Detective Sergeant Ted Williams was ringing the door bell on a smart Tudor style detached house. He sighed as he glanced at the portrait in the hallway of two children, an attractive girl in her early teens, and a slight bespectacled boy aged about ten.

"It appears that Mr Cooper went to the local pub for a couple of drinks before walking to the shopping centre. She got quite a shock when I arrived at the house."

"Thanks Ted. Fill in the paperwork, I'll check it later."

CHAPTER THIRTY

Inverness, April 1980

Thirteen years after the machete incident between the infant Davie Brown, and the adult Donnie Grey, there was a further confrontation between the two.

Although Donnie was more content than at any time in his life, he still felt bitter about his disfigurement, that had indirectly led to two years in prison.

Davie was celebrating his eighteenth birthday in the Ness Bar when the confrontation arose. Donnie had been with Shona for two years before he confessed that the scar had been caused by a five year old child.

Donnie and Davie had ignored each other completely during the thirteen year interval. But seeing Davie in the public house with friends, and seeing a young girl clinging to his arm, was too much for Donnie.

It could have been that Donnie had a little too much to drink. He had been in the bar for two hours, celebrating the birth of his son James Alexander. Shona and the new baby were expected to be in hospital for a few days, and Susan was staying with neighbours. It was the first time in six years that Donnie had been alone. He had not been in a public house in that time.

In front of a crowded bar, Donnie grabbed Davie by the throat. "Watch your back for the rest of your life. When you least expect it, I will be there. Your death will be very painful," he screamed into Davie's ear.

The following day Donnie received a visit from the police. They advised him that no charges were being pressed, but he was cautioned about his future behaviour.

***

Three months later Davie Brown was threatened again. When Danny Forsyth returned from a trip to his gangster associates in Glasgow a day earlier than expected, and found his wife Sharon in bed with Davie, both Davie and Sharon were hospitalised for a week. Only police intervention prevented murder.

For the second time in three months, Davie Brown heard the words "watch your back for the rest of your life" uttered in his ear.

Danny Forsyth was later sentenced to ten years imprisonment for attempted murder.

CHAPTER THIRTY ONE

Chatham, August 1980

Donnie Grey's confrontation with Davie Brown, and the resultant police caution, was the catalyst in Donnie and Shona making a life changing decision.

It had started innocently enough three months earlier when Shona was reminiscing about her childhood. Donnie also began reminiscing. Before they knew where the conversation was going, they were talking about the possibility of returning to the Medway towns.

It took three weeks to reach a final decision.

They calculated that the money from the sale of their home in Inverness, purchased from the lump sum death benefit Shona had received from Ian's employers, was sufficient capital to purchase a place to live in Medway. All that had to be resolved was work for Donnie.

"I don't see any problems," was Donnie's view. "It's a big enough area. If nothing else, there's always the Isle of Grain or even London."

***

Donnie gazed at the large office block and shopping complex occupying the space where The Eagle Tavern and The Bull had been.

"It's a monstrosity isn't it?"

Donnie looked at the man who had made the comment.

"It's called The Pentagon. They should have stuck the bloody thing in America. The place will never be occupied," continued the stranger.

"I see we have a new police station as well."

"It's all new around here, they've ripped the heart out of

Chatham, and all the work went to outside firms."

"Know something about building works do you?"

"A bit, I've got a small building company based in Chatham."

"Fancy a drink? I'm looking for work in the building trade?"

"That sounds good to me. I'm Charlie Fox."

Donnie followed Charlie Fox into the Chatham Arms.

"I own this doss house," said Charlie, "so don't complain about the beer."

Before Donnie got a chance to reply, Charlie Fox walked to the juke box. Donnie stood behind Charlie as he made his selections.

"Johnny Cash. Is that all you've got on this machine?"

"Don't be daft. There are a few Elvis records as well. Get me a pint of best bitter and we'll talk shop."

They were on their fourth drink when Charlie asked the question. "Out of curiosity how did you come by the scar?"

Donnie thought for moment. He saw no point in lying, but did not want to look a complete fool. "I got involved with a Scots nutter with a machete."

"Most of these Jocks are off their head. We have trouble every time they come into Chatham from the power station construction."

Donnie looked at his watch. "Christ, is that the time, Petty? I'd better get going. I told the wife I'd only be a couple of hours."

Charlie Fox looked at Donnie. "What did you just call me?"

Donnie paused for a moment. "I'm sorry. I wasn't thinking."

"Why Petty?"

"No offence meant. My mind tends to wander and, well you are on the small side. I just connected your size with your passion for Johnny Cash, and came up with the name Petty Cash."

Charlie rubbed his chin. "That's great. I like that. Petty

Cash. That's a helluva compliment." Charlie stood up. "See you on site first thing Monday. Good to meet you Donnie."

Charlie watched Donnie as he walked out of the bar.

Charlie had seen Donnie before. He wasn't sure where, but he knew he had seen him somewhere. He had the feeling it was in a bar somewhere. It was at the back of his mind.

He chuckled to himself. "Petty Cash. Brilliant."

***

Shona was pleased to hear that Donnie had found a job so quickly. That evening, once she had put baby James to bed, and talked with Susan about her homework tasks, she sat down.

She picked up the kitten they had just got for Susan. The kitten reminded her of her childhood.

CHAPTER THIRTY TWO

Hempstead, September 1980

"You're having me on aren't you?"

"Honestly Shona I'm not kidding. A flying saucer landed near here in the thirties."

"You're a chancer."

Donnie Grey looked at Shona and laughed. They were sitting in the lounge bar of the Flying Saucer public house, one mile from their new home in Rainham.

Donnie glanced around the bar. He heard the man before he saw him. He knew the voice. Donnie looked in the direction of the voice. He took a deep breath. He had not seen the man for sixteen years, but he was in no doubt. The memory of a knife sinking into soft flesh crossed his mind.

The man turned and stared at Donnie. A faint smile passed across the man's face.

"Let's finish our drink love. The baby-sitter will be wondering where we are," said Donnie.

Donnie held Shona closer to him as they walked to the car.

That night Donnie's nightmare returned. A white hand rising out of a dark abyss. He woke up sweating.

CHAPTER THIRTY THREE

Rainham, September 1980

Norman Bills could hear the knocking on his door. He looked at his bedside clock. It was only ten o'clock but Norman had been in bed for an hour. At the age of seventy he did not have much of a social life. There was little call for him to be out of bed after nine in the evening.

He wondered who could be calling so late at night. He had few visitors, and normally none after four o'clock in the afternoon. There were few people that he could tolerate. He had seen every aspect of life in his forty-five years in the medical profession. As far as Norman was concerned the human race was the pits.

Cursing to himself, Norman swung his legs out of bed. He picked up his dressing gown from the foot of the bed, and made his way downstairs, pausing briefly to finish the large whisky that was his normal bedtime tipple.

The knocking on the door stopped the moment Norman turned on the hall light.

Without a second thought Norman Bills, retired doctor and confirmed alcoholic, opened his front door. He had a brief glimpse of the person entering his house, holding what appeared to be a wooden mallet, before it struck him on the head. As he slumped to the floor he heard a voice whispering in his ear "That's for my little sister."

One minute after opening his front door he lay in a pool of blood at the foot of his stairs.

Norman Bills had finally overcome his drink problem.

CHAPTER THIRTY FOUR

Hempstead, September 1980

Donnie Grey leaned on the bar at the Flying Saucer. He checked his watch.

"Don't panic, I'm here," a voice whispered in his ear. "Get me a tonic water and bring it across to the corner table."

"Well, it's been a long time Donnie. It was quite a surprise seeing you in here the other evening, and an even bigger surprise when I got your call yesterday. So what's so urgent?"

Donnie looked at the man sitting opposite him. "I just want you to know that I've settled down now. I'm married and have a couple of kids. I'd hoped what happened all those years ago was in the past."

"It is as far as I am concerned, Donnie. Water under the bridge, life moves on etcetera."

"So I take it that I can forget about it?"

"I have. Why don't you just go home and forget about it. I trust you haven't mentioned it to anyone else." Donnie averted his gaze.

"Donnie…?"

"No. I haven't said a word to anyone."

"Right, we have nothing to worry about then, do we? But you must have upset someone judging by that scar on your face."

"It was an accident" said Donnie.

Donnie stopped at the door of the pub. He debated whether he should come clean with the man, and mention that he had told Andy Spiers.

Donnie turned round. The man he had been speaking to was on the public telephone.

He had already forgotten Donnie Grey.

CHAPTER THIRTY FIVE

London, June 1982

"It has the same pattern as the previous murder."

Billy Saunders looked up at the speaker.

"I can think of eight unsolved murders on the books. Which previous murder are you referring to?"

"Three months ago. Christie – the old chap who was strangled with a neck-tie in Shepherdess Walk. This victim has also been strangled with a neck-tie. It looks as though the body has been there a day or so."

Detective Inspector Billy Saunders raised himself out of his chair. He had been at Kings Cross police station for six months, following a two year spell at Scotland Yard. In that six months there had been forty murders. He expected to be at Kings Cross for a further eighteen months as part of the rotation system worked within the Met Police.

"Right, let's take a look."

Billy ducked under the police tent protecting the crime scene. In the glare of the portable task light he could see that the heavily built murdered man was in his fifties.

"Another businessman looking for a cheap thrill I suppose. Is there anything obvious missing?"

"No sign of a wallet, watch or jewellery. This looks odd though."

Billy bent down and looked at the sachet of powder being held by D.C. Perkins.

"I can't imagine that this was left here deliberately. It looks as though someone was doing a drugs and sex deal that went wrong. Let's get it to forensics, see if we can lift a print. In the meantime we check the local pubs to see if anyone recognises our businessman."

***

The barman at the Queens Arms looked at the photograph of the dead man. "I can't be certain. He looks different dead. But he may have been in here a couple of evenings ago. If it was him, he came in here once before."

"Was he alone?"

"He arrived alone on both occasions. I'm fairly sure that he left with one of the girls on the second occasion."

"One of the girls?"

"One of our regular customers, Annette. I think her surname is Scott."

"Describe her."

"Aged about forty, quite well dressed, lots of make-up."

"A working girl?"

"Not in the sense you mean. She is usually with a chap in a dark suit and a dark tie. This is a respectable pub."

***

"That barman's got to be joking hasn't he? Half the toms from the Pentonville Road were in there."

"Well, it could be a lead. Two murders involving a prostitute may not be just coincidence. I think it's time we checked with the Home Counties forces to see if they have experienced any similar incidents on their patch. I reckon it needed two people to carry out these killings. So far both victims have been on the well built side."

***

Twenty four hours later the fingerprints on the sachet of drugs were confirmed as those of Ann Stanton, a known prostitute.

"We have a photo from Chatham Police. It was taken seventeen years ago. The barman in the Queens Arms reckons she could be this Annette Scott. Let's circulate the photograph and see if we can track her down. For all we know the two bodies we have on this patch may just be the tip of the iceberg."

"We have an ID on the body. Leslie John Elison, age fifty-five, an accounts clerk from Bow. He has a record of importuning in a public toilet. He was a homosexual."

"So, it is unlikely that he was looking for sex with this Ann Stanton. Drugs appear to be the link."

"That's my guess."

"I think I'll give Chatham nick a call. I used to know a D.C. there in the sixties."

CHAPTER THIRTY SIX

Chatham, June 1982

Billy Saunders was greeted like a long lost friend when he met Ted Williams at Chatham Police Station. Ted Williams had also reached the rank of detective inspector.

"I don't know about you Ted, but I can't help feeling that the drugs bust we did in the sixties was a major factor in my promotion. The five years I did on the Central Drugs Squad was a huge boost to my career. It was a pity that the main man got away, but it was still a good result."

"It was. The drugs bust helped me a great deal as well. I have to admit that I envy you Billy. Life in the Met is quite a bit different from rural policing. Chatham has changed considerably since the sixties, and with the dockyard closing shortly I expect to see further changes in crime trends. You are stationed at Kings Cross now I gather. That must be quite a change from the Yard."

"There's much more variety. After five years on undercover work it seems a bit strange flashing a warrant and dealing with criminals other than just drug dealers. It's opened my eyes to a different side of the criminal mind. I had no idea that there were so many murders committed. We are averaging two murders a week on my patch. But even that is considerably lower than other Met areas."

"We have our fair share here. Most of them are the usual type, domestic violence getting out of hand, and we nail the culprit within a couple of hours. But we have a number of unsolved cases on our books," said Ted Williams.

"The ones I am particularly interested in discussing with you are two instances involving middle aged men, both strangled with a necktie. We found evidence at one of the scenes pointing to Ann Stanton, a prostitute from the

Chatham area in the sixties."

"Since your phone call I've made enquiries about Stanton. Apparently she left the Medway towns in the sixties, but she has been seen back in the towns on several occasions since then. She is well known to the beat bobbies as she has a record of violence. I've issued an instruction that she be apprehended on sight."

"I'm fairly certain that she had an accomplice in the Kings Cross murders, perhaps someone from the Chatham area. Did she have any associates?"

"None that spring to mind, but I'll make enquiries. Make no mistake, however, Stanton is wicked. I wouldn't be at all surprised if she was involved in some of the murders committed down here."

Ted Williams looked at his watch. "I've got a briefing just starting, but what are your plans for early evening? Why don't you come home and have dinner with the wife and I. She will be delighted to see you. When I said that an old Scotland Yard mate was visiting she was quite impressed."

"That sounds nice, Ted. It's been years since I had a meal in a family home. I never did get round to marrying. I'll let Kings Cross know where I am and keep my pager switched on just in case."

***

Billy Saunders glanced across the dining table and smiled at his hostess. Christine Williams was a vivacious brunette. In her late thirties to early forties Billy guessed. Ted and she appeared devoted to each other.

"How long have you two been married?"

Christine laughed. "I would have thought it was obvious. Only a month. The novelty hasn't worn off yet. Give Ted another six months and he'll lose the attentive touch."

Ted placed his hand on Christine's. "I've waited too long for you to lose my feelings that quickly, love."

"Have you never considered marriage, Billy?"

"Briefly, there was a girl once. I was nuts about her. But she didn't want me. Her parents quite liked me but they were opposed to marriage at the time."

"What happened to her?"

"We lost track of each other when she went into a different class room. We were only six at the time."

Christine roared with laughter. "Six years of age and in love. Now that is romantic."

"I can match that Billy. I was in love with Christine when I was six."

"In that case Ted I'll just keep hoping that my six year old comes back to me."

"Another drink?"

"I'll have the same as you, Ted."

"This is just mineral water."

"On second thoughts, it's a long drive back to north London. I'll just have a coffee. It would be embarrassing to be stopped whilst under the influence."

"Ted was saying that you are working on a murder case at the moment. I could do with some excitement in my life. Tell me all about it."

***

"And that's it Christine. Two unsolved murders, each a strangulation with a necktie, and with a strong lead to Ann Stanton. We'll get her eventually. It's just a matter of time. Now I really do have to go. It's been a super evening."

"The pleasure has been ours Billy. Come back one day with your child-hood sweetheart."

CHAPTER THIRTY SEVEN

London, July 1982

"Well that's it, Billy. We've had a consolidated report back from Kent Constabulary. There is no trace of Ann Stanton anywhere. They are now considering her as a serious suspect for several murders committed in the Chatham area in the past twenty years.

"Well we'll just have to keep looking. Have a word with the City police. They may have something on her."

***

Two days later the City of London Police, the independent body of police responsible for the financial square mile district, advised the Metropolitan Police that Ann Stanton was known in the City district as a high class hooker. She had been arrested six months previously for attacking one of her customers. The man she attacked had stated that she had a male accomplice. Charges against Ann Stanton had been dropped when the man who was assaulted, a director of a major city institution, refused to give any evidence for fear of embarrassment. As far as the City of London police were aware, Stanton and her accomplice had left the square mile.

CHAPTER THIRTY EIGHT

Gravesend – Kent, August 1982

Roy Gibson looked up as the tall man entered the lounge bar of the Dickens Hotel. He had been waiting over an hour. But he didn't mind waiting. The man he was meeting was important.

"The usual?"

"Yes please. Go easy on the ice though."

The tall man glanced around the room. It was as he had hoped. The room was deserted, which was hardly surprising considering the decor. It would have been no surprise to him if he had been told that Charles Dickens himself had sat in the same chair looking at the same wallpaper.

But the solitude and squalor suited the man. He needed a quiet, out of the way place to discuss business. What he wanted to talk about was very definitely illegal.

"Are we on target for the extra production?"

"Bang on. I've taken into account the loss of imports via the dockyard. We will suffer a loss in sales with the navy personnel moving out, but we are now geared to move into Essex, which will offset the naval sales."

"No. We stay in Kent. If we have to suffer a drop in revenue so be it. We would be taking risks if we operated out of the area."

"Well, if that's the way you want to run it."

"I laid down the rules from day one. Let's not spoil it now."

CHAPTER THIRTY NINE

Chatham, June 1986

Eric Anderton adjusted his jacket. Behind him was a hectic evening of home visits. What he needed was a drink. The public house lounge bar was packed as Eric made his way to the bar. "A large brandy please Stan, and take one for yourself."

"Thanks Eric. Busy day?"

"Bloody patients! Why can't they just turn up for surgery?"

An hour later, Eric Anderton was on his third brandy.

"Is that your pager I can hear?"

"Pager? Oh Christ, you're right." Eric Anderton looked at the message scrawled on his pager. "Jesus. Not her again."

"Another call out?"

"Just round the corner thank heavens. I can leave the car in the car park and walk home. I'll get my bag out of the car. Pop another brandy in there for me, Stan."

Eric Anderton cursed as he walked across the park. He could see the house he was visiting. He heard the voice behind him and turned.

"I'm sorry. What did you say?"

He felt the material pulling against his throat. He dropped his medicine bag. He put both hands on his neck in an effort to pull away the item strangling him. He felt the pressure in the middle of his back.

He fell to the ground. He did not feel the kicks inflicted.

***

The elderly man out walking his dog was attracted by the bleeping noise of a pager. The man had the sense not to remove the neck tie wrapped around Eric Anderton's throat.

CHAPTER FORTY

Inverness, May 1990

Twelve months after retiring from the Metropolitan Police, Billy Saunders was firmly entrenched back in his home town. The lump sum pension payment he had received on taking early retirement had enabled him to purchase a large chunk of the licensed trade. No fewer than five public houses in the town had the name William John Saunders above the door. He had managed to get the public houses at a good price. Even so, most of his lump sum payment had been swallowed up in the purchase of the businesses. Not that Billy needed much ready cash. With no wife or steady girlfriend to worry about his overheads were minimal. Golf twice a week and an expensive restaurant once a week were the extent of his vices.

"A fiver if you sink this one."

Billy looked at the five yard putt, on the ninth hole of the Culcabock Golf Course.

"Okay, you're on."

"Sod it," cursed Billy, as the ball rolled past the hole.

"I swear you're playing worse than you were a year ago."

"How's business. Had any good cases lately?"

Detective Inspector Sandy Burns of the Northern Constabulary was about to reply when his pager sounded.

Sandy slipped the pager back into his pocket. "Something's come up, a suspicious death at Clachnaharry. I'll have to break off."

"No problems. I'll get a taxi back to the town."

"Why don't you come along with me? We can have a drink later on. I'm sure the experience of an ex Inspector from Scotland Yard would be useful. If nothing else you may just get Lorna Reid off my back."

"Is she the new pathologist? I saw an article about her in

the Courier. She appears to be a bit of an expert on bodies, the older the better by all accounts."

"That's her. I just want to make sure she doesn't become an expert on my body. My wife can be quite possessive. But, as you say, she prefers old bodies, so that lets you in with a chance."

Billy drew himself up. At fifty-three he still held himself upright. A dark beard, lightly tinged with grey, set off his features. "I'm up for it. It'll be interesting to see a crime scene again."

***

"Archie Stokes is his name. Aged about sixty, a bachelor, he lived on his own. He was a well respected businessman, semi-retired, but worked for various charities. He was also a local councillor and quite high up on the planning and development committee," reeled off Sandy Burns.

"You knew him then."

"Only in passing. I met him at some of the police functions."

"Any relatives?"

"A younger brother in Australia I believe."

Billy held the handkerchief over his mouth, and looked at the body. "This is a vicious assault by any standards. Whoever did this certainly meant to kill him."

***

"I would say that he's been dead for over a week," stated Lorna Reid. "I'll know better back at the mortuary."

"Thanks, and cause of death?"

"Bloody obvious I would think, even to a thick copper. His head has been smashed in by a heavy object, and if I'm not mistaken the heavy object is by the window."

Sandy looked at Lorna. In her mid forties, she was a very

attractive woman. He brought his mind back to matters in hand, and looked at the object which lay on the floor underneath a broken window.

"It looks like a piece of marble Billy, and there is blood, hair, and I dread to think what else on it."

Sandy bent down among the broken glass.

"Found something?"

"A signet ring, doesn't look expensive, with the initials EJ."

"Let's have a look."

Billy peered at the ring. "I've seen this before."

"Don't be a smart arse Billy."

"Seriously, this ring belongs to one of my customers. I can't think which customer, or which pub, but I'll make enquiries."

"Well it's clearly a break-in. It'll be difficult to know if anything has been taken as Stokes lived on his own."

"I think we can assume that there had been a video recorder there," stated Billy, pointing to an area close to a television set. "You can see by the surrounding dust where an object has been resting. It doesn't look as though Mr Stokes was too fond of housekeeping."

"It looks as though something has been removed from the ledge above the fireplace, possibly a picture or a clock."

"So it looks like an interrupted burglary."

"That would be my guess."

Billy Saunders bent down and looked closely at the piece of marble. "It could be a marble paperweight, although I've never seen one this shape and size before. Probably weighs a couple of pounds. Small, but obviously lethal."

Enquiries later that day at the charity organisations that Archie Stokes had been involved with, revealed that he had not been seen for over a week. There was nothing unusual in this however. Archie Stokes had no fixed routine with the charities.

In an effort to pin-point a more accurate last sighting of Stokes, police officers interviewed several of the local town councillors. These enquiries revealed that he had failed to turn up for a council committee meeting eight days earlier. When he missed a further meeting seven days later, one of the councillors suggested that a visit be made to Stokes' home. It was then the body was discovered.

CHAPTER FORTY ONE

Inverness, May 1990

Billy Saunders arrived back in the Auld Lang Syne to be given the news that his bar manager at the Merkinch Arms had a problem. Thirty minutes later Billy discovered what the problem was. A funeral wake was in progress, and the mourners were getting out of hand.

"Who died?"

"Eddie Jackson. He was found dead in his bed five days ago by his young son."

"That's it" exclaimed Billy, recalling where he had seen the signet ring before. He had ejected Eddie Jackson from the Merkinch Arms the previous month for trying to sell stolen goods in the pub.

***

"I've found the owner of the ring," Billy informed Sandy Burns five minutes later. "But I'm afraid you're going to have a problem getting a confession from him."

He outlined the problem regarding a confession.

"Am I to understand that Jackson's relatives and neighbours are in the Merkinch Arms at the moment?"

"Half the district are here. Why do you ask?"

"I'll come back to you."

***

Two hours later Sandy Burns contacted Billy Saunders. Eddie Jackson was well known to the police. A discreet police search of Jackson's house, undertaken whilst his wake was in progress, had uncovered a quantity of stolen goods including a video recorder and a photograph of a country scene in a silver photo frame. The frame was identical to one seen in Stokes' house. The country scene was the view from Stokes' rear garden.

"We've removed the video and photograph. There's a strong chance that we will find Stokes' fingerprints on the video recorder. It's fairly obvious the photograph was stolen from his house."

The following day Sandy confirmed that Stokes' prints were on the two items retrieved from Eddie Jackson's house. Of even greater importance was the news that Eddie Jackson's prints were on the piece of marble used as the murder weapon.

"What I can't understand" said Sandy, "is that Jackson has no record of violence. Killing Stokes is totally out of character."

Billy switched off his phone. He was thoughtful.

"What type of burglar" he asked himself, "removes items from a house, and leaves behind a murder weapon?"

Billy's thinking was interrupted a few minutes later when he went into the bar of Auld Lang Syne prior to going out to dinner – a dinner for one.

Standing at the bar, dressed to kill, was Lorna Reid. "I've phoned the restaurant and changed the reservation to dinner for two," she said.

***

It was three hours later, over brandy, that Lorna dropped the bombshell. "I've deliberately stayed off the subject of work all evening. But I think there is something you may be interested to know. The killing of Archie Stokes was not quite as straight-forward as first appeared."

"In what way?"

"The item found at the scene, the piece of marble with blood, hair and half of Stokes' brains on it, was not the murder weapon. The marble had been gouged into Stokes' head after his death."

CHAPTER FORTY TWO

Inverness, May 1990

The following week Billy Saunders and Lorna Reid attended the Police Ball together, raising a few eyebrows with their presence. Billy was fascinated with Lorna's tales of life in New Zealand. He was disappointed to hear that she would only be in Inverness for two years as she was on a temporary exchange posting.

Lorna was equally fascinated with tales of Billy's life in the Metropolitan Police. When he later related tales of his childhood, of growing up in Inverness in the forties and the fifties, she fell about laughing.

"Do you honestly mean to say that you spent part of your childhood going around the town on a horse and cart with your grandfather, collecting scraps of food for his pig farm."

"The other kids called me 'smelly'. Bath night was Sunday night in a tin tub. It was fine in the early part of the week and in the winter. But in summer, when I helped grandad in the evenings at the pig farm, I used to smell terrible the next day. I never did have much luck with the girls."

"I'm sure you've made up for it since then."

"Women have never bothered me. The job always came first. There was one lass, she's been around in my head for over forty years. They say you never forget your first love."

"You retired from the force quite young, any reason?"

"Disillusionment I suppose, and a hankering to come home. I could never take to the bureaucracy of higher office. Promotion to Chief Inspector was offered, but it would have meant being stuck in an office. Not my scene I'm afraid. "

Billy looked around the room. The Police Ball was well attended. "Do you know many people here, Lorna?"

"A few of them. The crowd on the next table are local councillors. You know Provost Anderson of course. Next to him are Councillors Roberts, Stephens, MacKay and Leslie. I assume the women with them are their wives. The people on the table behind them are members of the Rotary Club, including Jack Ellis, the Highland Development Board Chairman."

Billy glanced at the tables as Lorna reeled off the names. One face seemed familiar, a face from his past. But a face he could not place.

"Right, let's raise a few eyebrows and dance."

As Billy Saunders and Lorna Reid tripped the light fantastic, they were keenly watched by those looking for signs that the relationship was more than just professional.

They were unaware that two of the observers were not the least bit interested in any signs of romance.

Their interest was much more personal – murder.

CHAPTER FORTY THREE

Inverness, August 1990

When Lorna Reid was selected for the exchange posting position she immediately contacted property agents in Inverness to determine the availability of furnished rented accommodation in the area. The moment she saw the letting details on the small cottage overlooking Loch Ness, she fell in love with it.

She had Billy Saunders on her mind as she drove across the Caledonian Canal on her way to Eden Court Theatre. They had seen a great deal of each other since the Police Ball three months earlier. She found Billy's company stimulating. At forty two years of age she was beginning to realise that it was time to settle down. Billy was no spring chicken, but he had more going for him than any man she had met in the previous ten years. She laughed inwardly as she imagined the extent of gossip doing the rounds of the town's business community.

She glanced at the cemetery as she passed. Billy had explained to her what the Gaelic word Tomnahurich meant – the Hill of the Fairies. He had added that the cemetery was listed as one of the most beautiful in the world – a statement that Lorna thought was probably true.

Lorna was fifty yards past the cemetery when she braked. She sat in the car for the next five minutes. The more she thought about it the more obvious the answer was.

The investigation into the murder of Archie Stokes had ground to a halt. A police search of Eddie Jackson's house had revealed no sign of a murder weapon. But she was now certain she knew exactly what had been used to brutalise Archie Stokes.

She checked her watch. It was seven thirty. She had half

an hour before she was due at the theatre, where she was giving a lecture on pathology to the Ladies Institute.

"Be there Billy," she muttered to herself, counting her blessings that the telephone-box at the entrance to the cemetery was working.

"Bloody answering machines," she exclaimed, slamming the telephone receiver down. She sat for a moment. It would be easy enough to confirm her suspicions. Five minutes later she drew up in the theatre car park.

"Do you have a list of people attending the lecture?"

The receptionist looked up at the sound of Lorna's voice. "I have a copy right here."

"Thanks, Gloria. Did you enjoy the ceilidh last night?"

"Apart from that bloody husband of mine getting drunk and making a fool of himself. What is it with men, drink, and barmaids?"

Lorna laughed and glanced at the list of attendees. The numbers had been restricted to fifty. It was encouraging to note that all the tickets had been taken. The hospital charity would benefit.

She spotted the name she was looking for: Karen Gregory. She checked her watch. Ten minutes to eight. There was time to speak to Karen before her lecture. She checked the coffee shop, the obvious place for Karen to be.

"Anyone seen Karen?" she called to a throng of women.

"I don't think Karen has arrived yet. Can I help in any way?"

"Of course, I'd forgotten about you Annie, you'll know the answer just as well as Karen," replied Lorna, looking at Annie Stephens, the treasurer of the Institute. In her fifties, Annie had been a founding member of the Ladies Institute along with Karen Gregory.

Five minutes later, using the theatre office telephone, Lorna phoned Billy Saunders. She left a message on his answering machine. Her reasoning had been correct. She needed to speak to him urgently.

***

Lorna cast her professional eye over the set-up. It was evident that no expense had been spared in the fitting out. She decided that she would visit Billy as soon as she was free. It was late, and she had the journey home to the cottage to face after seeing Billy. She smiled to herself. Tonight may just be the night that she and Billy would finally hit it off. Perhaps she may not have to drive home after all.

Speaking to Annie had confirmed her suspicions. She picked the object up. It was exactly as she suspected. A piece of marble had been used to murder Stokes. But not the piece found at the scene.

She checked her watch. She had been on her own for two minutes. She gazed into the open drawer out of idle curiosity. She looked at the collection of watches, rings and jewellery. She turned as she heard the noise behind her. She was too late. The scarf was already cutting off her breath.

CHAPTER FORTY FOUR

Inverness, August 1990

Billy Saunders listened once again to the message that Lorna had recorded three hours earlier.

"The moment you get this please call me. I think I've learned something useful about the murder of Archie Stokes."

The second message had been left thirty minutes after the first. "I'm just going into a lecture now. I'll contact you later. It's important."

Billy had arrived back at his flat ten minutes earlier, having spent the evening at a golf club dinner. He had tried Lorna as soon as he had got home. There had been no answer to his call. He wondered what she had found out.

Billy snatched the telephone from the cradle after the second ring.

"Lorna?"

"It's Sandy Burns. Can you meet me in Queensgate straight away?"

"What's up?"

"I'll let you know when you get here."

***

The police tape was stretched across the entrance to Queensgate. Billy parked his car and walked across to a police officer standing at the entrance to the street.

"I'm here to see Inspector Burns."

The officer raised the tape. "He's down there on the right, beside the police car."

"What's up?"

"I'll let the inspector tell you, sir."

Sandy Burns looked up as he saw Billy approaching.

"Bad news I'm afraid, Billy."

"What type of bad news?"

"It's Lorna. She's been murdered."

***

"Strangled. By the looks of it"

"It appears that way. A passer by noticed her slumped over the wheel of her car and knocked on the window. He then called us. It happened fairly recently."

Billy looked closely at the cloth around Lorna's neck. "It's her own scarf. I was with her when she bought it last week." Billy leaned further into the car. "There's a strange smell here, very faint, but noticeable, even above Lorna's perfume."

"What type of smell?"

"I'm not sure. It reminds me of death for some reason, but Lorna's perfume confuses me."

"SOCO will be here shortly. They will carry out a good search. Have you any idea where Lorna was tonight?"

"She was giving a lecture to the Ladies' Institute at the Eden Court Theatre. She left a couple of messages on my answering machine."

"Anything of importance?"

"It certainly seems that way now. She said she had some information on Archie Stokes' murder."

CHAPTER FORTY FIVE

Inverness, August 1990

Two weeks later Sandy Burns contacted Billy Saunders. .

"We're no further forward in the investigation I'm afraid. We've eliminated all the prints found in the car. We've also interviewed most of the women who attended the lecture. She spoke to a few of the women during the course of the evening. In each case the conversation was just general chit chat, apart from a discussion she had with the treasurer Annie Stephens. Mrs Stephens reports that Lorna had asked her if any member of the Ladies Institute had ever reported being accosted by Archie Stokes. Mrs Stephens thought the question was rather odd. It appears that Lorna was actually looking for Karen Gregory Mrs Gregory states she did not speak to Lorna. Nobody saw Lorna leave the theatre.

"Was Stokes ever the subject of a complaint to the police?"

"Several years ago one of his neighbours complained about Peeping Tom activities in the area. Stokes and other men in the area were interviewed as a matter of routine, but nothing was ever proven."

"And you have no idea what Lorna was doing in Queensgate?"

"It's a complete mystery, Billy. All the businesses in Queensgate are closed at that time of night."

"So that's it then. We've come to a dead end."

"For the time being. We will keep the case open of course. Something may break."

"Will you be at the funeral service tomorrow?"

"Yes, I'll be there. I believe her parents are arriving from New Zealand to take her ashes back. Will you be meeting them?"

"I have arranged to pick them up at the airport. Phoning them about Lorna's death was one of the most difficult things I've ever done. She and I got quite close in a short period of time."

"She was quite a girl, Billy."

CHAPTER FORTY SIX

Chatham, February 1995

Extract from the Chatham Gazette dated 10 February 1995

DOCTOR MURDERED IN CAR PARK

The body of fifty-nine year old Chatham doctor Andrew Harris was discovered in Chatham Library car park late yesterday.

Detective Inspector Arthur Mason, based at Chatham Police Station, advises the Gazette that Dr. Harris was strangled with a necktie.

Dr. Harris had been at the Chatham Conservative Club earlier in the evening where he had given a talk on the role of General Practitioners in the Health Service. Dr Harris is well known within political circles for his outspoken views on the need for General Practitioners to discontinue home visits and to be on a controlled working week.

In an identical murder in June 1986 the body of Dr Eric Anderton was found in a playing field at Hempstead.

Detective Inspector Mason confirms that the police are looking into the possibility of a connection between the two murders.

CHAPTER FORTY SEVEN

Inverness, July 1995

Thirty-six year old Jimmie Brown was concerned. Jimmie drank, womanised, gambled, dipped into fraudulent activities, and occasionally executed the odd burglary with his father Tommy and brother Davie. On an actuarial chart, most of Jimmie's life was still ahead of him. But Jimmie's concern was not how long he would live; whether he ever married; if he would find long term employment; or even his current girlfriend.

His concern was his father, who had had retired two years earlier. Tommy had financed his retirement by selling his share of the Salah and Brown removals business. When Peter Salah started ducking and diving with the tax man, Tommy decided to get out of the business. Tommy normally had no qualms about cheating the revenue people, but Peter's scams were obvious. Tommy had got a fair price for his share of the partnership, but the horses, drink, and his long term girlfriend Irene Norman, had taken care of his windfall. At the age of fifty-six Tommy was flat broke with no pension and no prospect of any income. Even his burglary career had come to an end because of a recurring back problem.

Jimmie gazed at the blank computer screen in front of him. He had been with Glentorry Oil Company for six months. The previous week he had been advised that Glentorry had been bought out by North Sea Oil, the biggest oil company in the western hemisphere. Jimmie was about to be made redundant.

He looked back on his work career since leaving school. He had held three jobs and executed a total of four years in work in sixteen years. When not in legally paid employment he had fiddled the social security, carried out odd jobs for cash in hand, executed other nefarious activities, and studied computing at evening classes.

The thought of redundancy did not bother Jimmie. He could rise above such petty inconveniences. Although it was a pity, as he had been enjoying his time at Glentorry as a statistics clerk in the personnel data centre.

He picked up the document that his line manager had placed in front of him. Headed "Confidential", the document listed the company pension details of the three hundred and six Glentorry pensioners who were being absorbed into the much larger North Sea Oil pension scheme. The individual hard copy file for each pensioner had been forwarded to North Sea Oil the previous week.

Jimmie scanned the list. A footnote caught his eye.

"Please note that Mr Hamish MacGregor, formerly the manager of the Aberdeen branch, died on 5 July 1995. Pension payments detailed at line 229 above, and previously advised by hard copy should be ignored. There are no named beneficiaries to the estate of Mr MacGregor. This file should be closed and all pension payments terminated."

***

Two hours later Jimmie completed transmitting the details of the pensions. Confirmation of receipt was acknowledged by the Group Pension Scheme manager at North Sea Oil. The manager confirmed that pension payments under the new scheme would commence on 1st of August.

Line 229, indicated that Mr Hamish MacGregor had a pension benefit of twelve thousand two hundred and six pounds a year. A revised footnote indicated a change in the bank details of Mr MacGregor, and a change of address. His new address was given as 203 Craigton Avenue, Inverness.

The following day Tommy Brown visited the Nelson Street branch of the Bank of Scotland. He handed in a request for an additional account holder to be added to his current account. The name of the additional account holder was Mr Hamish MacGregor, who had been in retirement five years, but had decided, at the age of seventy, to move to Inverness. Tommy advised the bank that Mr MacGregor was his cousin.

The bank was delighted to receive the additional business.

Tommy Brown now had a steady income for the rest of his life.

CHAPTER FORTY EIGHT

Inverness, April 1998

Davie Brown had checked out the house several times over the previous month. He knew there was a chance that the house would be occupied. The house was big, and the owners were in the habit of leaving the lights on even when the house was empty.

He had been waiting thirty minutes before he made his move. Lights were on in one of the first floor bedrooms, and in the kitchen area at the rear of the house.

It took him two minutes to prise open the garage door. He knew that he could access the house direct from the garage. He had made several deliveries of furniture to the house six years earlier, with his father and Peter Salah.

The master bedroom would have been the ideal place to look for valuables, but seeing the light on in that area made him wary. The study, located at the front of the house, was the next likely source.

***

Davie tried the first key in the lock. Nothing. He tried the next key. Still nothing. He had eight keys left to try. He had bought the set of master keys from a contact in the Harbour Inn. On ten jobs to date he had come up trumps each time.

The lock turned. Davie gently pulled open the top drawer of the bureau. He was so intent in looking at the contents of the bureau that it took him a second to realise that someone had turned on the study light.

"Davie? What the hell are you doing here?"

Davie turned round. "I would think it's bloody obvious what I'm doing. More to the point what the hell are you doing? There must be thousands of pounds here."

"Seventy four thousand to be precise," replied the house owner calmly.

Davie looked again at the money.

One hour later Davie shook hands with the owner of the house. In return for his silence Davie was to become a partner in the business.

CHAPTER FORTY NINE

Inverness, November 2000

Police Constable David Lennox, who was manning the enquiries desk at Inverness Police Station, was having difficulty explaining to the distressed elderly man at the enquiries counter that the fact that his thirty eight year old son had not come home for three nights did not necessarily mean that something sinister had happened to him.

"I can assure you sir that half the men in this town disappear for days at a time but their wives don't complain. They're only too glad."

"That's enough Lennox. I'll take over here" interjected Sergeant MacBain, making a mental note to speak to the inspector about PC Lennox.

"Right sir, what appears to be the problem?"

"My son has not come home for three days"

"Is that unusual? Could he be staying with a friend?"

"He has no friends. Staying away from home is totally out of character. He came home three nights ago in a distressed state after having been involved in a scuffle in the Raigmore Tavern. He said he was going back out, and here I quote him, 'to sort someone out'. I have not seen him since then."

"Right, give me all the details."

***

"I'm very foolishly going to leave you in charge here Lennox whilst I visit the Raigmore Tavern. Do you think you can hold the fort without upsetting too many members of the public?" growled Sergeant MacBain.

CHAPTER FIFTY

Inverness

"Well that puts a different light on matters." Sergeant MacBain looked at PC Sandy Barnes, who had accompanied him to the Raigmore Tavern.

"It appears that a violent threat was made against Terry Thornton three nights ago by someone called Tommy Brown. The bar manager says no blows were exchanged, but Brown threatened to kill Thornton. I think we'll pay Brown a visit. The manager believes he lives in the Ferry district."

"203 Craigton Avenue, if memory serves me right," stated Constable Barnes. "He's well known to us is Mr Brown. No form, but he sails close to the wind. He was involved with a dodgy removals company. Rumour has it that he and his sons have been defrauding the social security for years, but they've never found any evidence against them."

Five minutes later, PC Barnes drew to a halt outside 203 Craigton Avenue. The moment the car stopped it was surrounded by a group of scruffy children.

"Sit on the bonnet of this car Barnes, and don't let anyone within ten yards of it," ordered the sergeant.

There was no reply to Sergeant MacBain's pounding on the door of no 203.

A small child glared at the sergeant.

"There's no one in the house, old man Brown's probably with his fancy piece, Jimmie's drunk in the Harbour Inn, and Davie's in Spain."

The sergeant looked at the street urchin. The toerag only looked about five years old.

"Make a note of his name, Barnes. He looks like a future customer."

The child stuck two fingers in the air as he dropped the

brick he was carrying on the roof of the police car.

***

Three minutes later, having scattered a group of school children crossing the main road, the police car drew up outside 186b Grant Street. Before Sergeant MacBain got a chance to knock, the door flew open.

"Is it Tommy? What's he been up to?" screamed a red haired blousy woman of indeterminate age.

Sergeant MacBain blew cigarette smoke away from his face. "I take it you are Mrs Irene Norman, and you are referring to Thomas Brown."

"Referring to him? I'll kill the bastard next time I see him. He's been like a bear with a sore head for the last three days. If he's got another woman I'll kill him."

"Calm down, love. Let's go indoors."

"Sod off you nosey little buggers," shouted Irene Norman to four small children who were clambering over the police car. Sergeant MacBain looked around for Constable Barnes. The bare-headed constable was fifty yards away, in hot pursuit of a small child who was kicking a police helmet as he ran.

It took ten minutes, and a flood of tears from Irene Norman, before Sergeant MacBain got the full story. She related how Tommy Brown had arrived at her home three nights earlier in a dishevelled state wearing a jacket covered in blood. Each evening since then he had arrived at her home in a foul mood. When she tackled him about his mood he said that he was worried about his son Davie. He did not elaborate on the cause of his concern about Davie.

"Is he in any sort of trouble?"

The sergeant was about to respond to Irene's question when the front door of the house opened.

Tommy Brown walked in. He had a bruise on his face and a cut on his cheek. He sustained a further bruise when Irene Norman hit him with a left hook.

Sergeant MacBain dragged her off Tommy Brown.

Tommy stood in the doorway, panting.

"You seem to have been in a bit of bother, Mr Brown."

"I can handle her."

"I'm not talking about Mrs Norman. I mean the bruising, and the cut on your face."

"I was attacked three nights ago. Some kid struck me from behind. I retaliated, but he caught me in the face. Mind you, I gave him a right bloody nose."

"Any idea who it was?"

"No. I didn't get a good look at him."

"Were you in the Raigmore Tavern three nights ago?"

Tommy Brown pondered. "I think I was. I've been in so many pubs in the last three days that I'm not too sure."

"I'd like to see the clothes you were wearing three nights ago?"

"I'm still wearing them. I'm usually very fussy, but I haven't been home for several days. I only keep a few clothes here."

Sergeant MacBain looked at the jacket Tommy was wearing. "Are you sure that was the jacket you were wearing three nights ago?"

Tommy looked at his jacket. "I'm not sure now. It may have been. If it wasn't, the jacket I was wearing will be in Irene's bedroom."

Sergeant MacBain looked at Irene Norman. "Would you mind fetching the jacket?"

***

The sergeant looked at the dark stain across the front of the jacket that Irene had produced. "Is this the jacket you wore three nights ago?"

"Yes. I remember now. It was in a bit of a mess so I changed jackets."

"This looks like blood to me. Do you happen to know Terence Thornton."

"I've never heard of him."

"I'd like you to accompany me to the station. You may wish to contact your solicitor."

Twenty four hours later Tommy Brown was advised that he was being detained on suspicion of murder. The dark stains on his jacket were confirmed as type O Positive, the same blood group as Terry Thornton. Tommy Brown was blood group AB.

CHAPTER FIFTY ONE

Inverness

Tommy Brown looked up as his cell door opened. He had been in Porterfield Prison for six days and had reached the end of his tether. He was physically and emotionally drained from exhaustive questioning on the whereabouts of Terry Thornton. Despite his vehement denials that he had not touched Terry Thornton, the police made it clear that they were proceeding with the murder charge.

"You have a visitor."

"Any idea who it is?"

The warder shrugged.

"Get off your backside and you'll find out."

Tommy walked into the visitors' reception room escorted by the warder. Twenty of the thirty interview tables were in use.

"Over there," the warder stated. Tommy glanced across the room, looking for a familiar face. "There," the warder pointed.

Tommy looked in the direction indicated. A tall man rose from his chair, and waved at Tommy.

"Tommy, old mate, it's good to see you again after all this time," said the man, pumping Tommy's hand.

"What the hell are you doing here? It must be more than twenty years since I've seen you."

"Sit down, Tommy, and don't say a word. Just listen to what I have to say."

Fifteen minutes later a bemused Tommy Brown was escorted back to his cell.

The following day a solicitor arrived at the prison and requested an interview with the prison governor.

Thirty minutes after the solicitor departed Tommy was

visited by the prison chaplain who advised Tommy that his son Jimmie had died of a heart attack the previous day. Tommy was asked what the funeral arrangements should be.

CHAPTER FIFTY TWO

Inverness

The drone of bagpipes playing a lament could be heard throughout the Ferry district as the funeral procession for Jimmie Brown got under way. Tommy Brown had decreed years earlier that he wanted a traditional Ferry funeral when he passed on. Tommy was a real 'Man of the Ferry', and believed in tradition. Loading his coffin into a hearse at his front door and taking it direct to a hole in the ground at the cemetery was too simple for Tommy. He wanted style when he passed on. What Tommy had not anticipated was that one of his sons would predecease him. But when the prison chaplain informed him of Jimmie's death, Tommy made his wishes known. Jimmie was to have a traditional Ferry funeral.

The sound of the bagpipes brought neighbours rushing into the street, as the piper manoeuvred himself through the doorway of Jimmie's home. In the time honoured ritual for a man leaving the Ferry on his final journey, the coffin, carried by six men from the Ferry, followed the piper as the procession began its half mile journey to the Citadel Church. All the neighbours followed the coffin. The wail of the bagpipes was matched by the wails from a heavily pregnant Elsie Rooney, the late Jimmie Brown's girlfriend.

Flanking one of the pall bearers, and looking out of place in an immaculately pressed prison uniform, was an officer from HM Prison Porterfield. The glint of metal, from the handcuffs attached to the pallbearer, was an indication that the officer was there in an official capacity.

According to his neighbours, Jimmie Brown, at the age of forty, had died peacefully in his sleep. The neighbours unanimously agreed that it was unlikely that the cardiac arrest could be attributed to hard work. Since being made redundant five years earlier, Jimmie had spent most of his time at evening classes improving his computer skills, or at the dole office.

An hour after departing his family home for the last time, and with the funeral service complete, Jimmie began his final journey to Tomnahurich Cemetery. Members of the Brown family had been buried there for generations. Seated in the lead funeral car following the hearse was Irene Norman. The last time Irene had been this close to Jimmie was when she had given birth to him.

Davie Brown, dressed in summer clothing, looked out of place amidst the mourners. He had been in Costa Del Sol when he received the news that Jimmie was dead. Davie had arrived back too late for the Citadel service, as his taxi from Inverness Airport had been held up in traffic. He arrived at his family home to be greeted with the news that the service at the Citadel church was over, and the funeral party were at the cemetery. Dropping his suitcase in the hallway, Davie got back in the taxi. There had been no time to change into more sensible winter clothing. Not that he felt the cold. Jimmie and Davie had been close, and the news of his older brother's demise had hit Davie badly. Seeing his father in handcuffs had added to his shock. The harsh winter cold would hit his bones when the shock off the day's events wore off, and reality set in.

The swirling snow at the graveside brought the mourners huddling together in an effort to keep out the bitter cold from the northerly wind which was sweeping across the gravestones.

The minister said his final few words. The prison officer reluctantly removed the handcuffs from the wrist of Tommy Brown, in order that Tommy could assist in lowering his son's casket into the dark hole in the ground.

Davie took one last look at the coffin as it settled into the grave. Ferry men were not supposed to cry, but the loss of a brother was a step too far to conform to macho rules.

The pall bearers withdrew the ropes from the coffin.

The pall bearer at the rear of the left flank of three Ferry men turned.

Davie looked at him. The Ferry was a close knit community. He would know all the men carrying his brother's coffin, but the scarf wrapped around the lower half of the pall bearer's face to keep out the bitter cold hid his face from view.

The sound of a mobile telephone broke the graveyard silence. Heads turned, as the mourners sought to identify where the sound came from.

Davie hastily dug into his trouser pocket. Turning away from the funeral party, he spoke softly into the telephone. "Whoever this is, you've picked the bloody wrong time. I'm just burying my brother. Call back later."

"For heavens sake Davie don't hang up. Never mind the funeral, get me out of here, I'm suffocating," the voice of Davie's dead brother Jimmie screamed in his ear.

A gust of wind blew the scarf from the face of the pall bearer. Davie stared in disbelief.

Davie collapsed.

The minister turned away from the grave, just in time to see Davie fall to the ground.

The noise of his fall prompted the other mourners to turn around. They turned around yet again, as the roar of an engine broke the silence of the graveyard.

Tommy Brown was in the passenger seat of the hearse as it sped out of the cemetery. The driver of the hearse was the masked pall bearer.

In the meantime the prison officer was attempting to climb out of the grave. A position he had assumed following a nudge from one of the mourners.

CHAPTER FIFTY THREE

Inverness

Five minutes after leaving the cemetery the hearse pulled outside Jimmie Brown's house. Tommy Brown and his escape accomplice, the masked pall bearer- the instigator of Davie's faint – although it could be argued that Jimmie's voice from the grave had more effect on Davie – sprinted into the house. They knew that, within minutes, the police would be at the house. Time was of the essence. Sitting outside the house was their new getaway vehicle, a cream coloured transit van bearing the name P. Salah – Removals.

Had Tommy Brown ever had the opportunity to sell his council house, he would almost certainly have listed the main feature of the property as the walk in wardrobe, which he had installed to hold his large collection of trendy gear. Even though he was in his early sixties, Tommy had a taste in stylish clothing that would have done credit to a teenage pop idol. The question of selling the property was unlikely to arise however as Tommy still rented the property from the local council. On being offered the opportunity to purchase the house, under the right to buy scheme, Tommy had made it quite clear to the council that it was "their bloody council house, and they would continue repairing it." As far as Tommy was concerned he was working class, and the working class lived in council houses.

A loud banging noise could be heard from the wardrobe as Tommy ran into his bedroom. He pulled on the handle of the wardrobe door. It would not open.

Tommy did not hesitate. He kicked the wardrobe door as hard as he could. The door buckled in the centre, and the left hand door swung out, whilst the right hand door swung in.

The left door caught Tommy full in the face. He yelped

in pain. The right door caught Jimmie Brown on the head as he fell out of the wardrobe gasping for breath. His mobile phone was clutched in his hand.

"As fast as you can, Jimmie. The police will be here soon. We've got to move sharply." Tommy pulled open a bedside cabinet. His mobile telephone was where he had left it fourteen days earlier.

"There's a suitcase downstairs packed with clothes and shaving kit," Jimmie stated.

Followed by Tommy, Jimmie sprinted down the stairs, heading for the front door.

"Just out of curiosity Jimmie, what were you doing in the wardrobe?"

"I thought I'd better hide away in case someone entered the house during the funeral. As it was, I did hear someone come in the house, but they left almost immediately."

The pall bearer was two yards ahead of the others by the time he reached the van. Tommy picked up a letter which lay on a small table inside the front door with one hand, and the suitcase with the other hand. The suitcase full of clothing had been good thinking on Jimmie's part.

Tommy threw the case into the back of the van, slammed the door shut, and threw himself into the passenger seat. There was barely enough room for the three of them.

The van accelerated out of Craigton Avenue. Five minutes later the van was on the A9 heading south.

Ninety minutes away from Inverness the pall bearer removed the scarf from his face and grinned broadly. Then he laughed out loud as he recalled the look on Davie Brown's face at the cemetery.

It was hardly surprising that Davie had fainted. Davie had probably been dreading the moment he met Donnie Grey again. Davie had been in no doubt that Donnie meant it when twenty years earlier he said he would kill him if he ever saw him again.

In deep thought, Donnie Grey touched the scar on his face.

CHAPTER FIFTY FOUR

Inverness

At the same time as Donnie Grey was in the getaway vehicle recollecting his various encounters with Davie Brown, a scruffy man of indeterminable age, wearing a torn anorak, faded jeans, and trainers, was approaching the Craigton Avenue residence of the Brown family. The visitor cautiously pulled his cap over his face as he neared the house. He looked just like ninety per cent of the local male population.

He waited thirty minutes following the police departure. The police search of the house had taken an hour. The visitor smiled as he saw the result of the search – a polythene evidence bag carried by a plain clothes officer.

The visitor pulled his anorak around him and walked up the path. The same path that the piper had trod as he stage managed Jimmie Brown's departure to the next world.

The stranger pushed open the unlocked door and entered the house.

It took him ten minutes to convince himself that the suitcase that Davie Brown had brought back from Spain was not in the house. There was a suitcase there, but not the one that Davie had taken to Spain. The suitcase, which was in the house, contained clean clothing and shaving kit.

This left the visitor with a major problem.

Where was Davie's suitcase?

CHAPTER FIFTY FIVE

A1 Southbound

Tommy Brown wiped the egg from his plate with a piece of bread, and looked at his son Jimmie and Donnie Grey. They had parked overnight in a forest track three miles south of Perth. Since then they had travelled nonstop for six hours, and the strain was showing. The food at the Little Chef on the M1 thirty miles from London, was palatable, certainly better than the food that Tommy had become accustomed to in his brief stay in prison.

"A toast," said Jimmie, picking up his mug of tea, "to the future."

Tommy acknowledged the toast. "Well it's all gone right so far. A brilliant plan Donnie, well done." Donnie Grey shrugged his shoulders. "Don't be so modest. It took some planning," continued Tommy. "It's only thanks to you, that I'm no longer in prison for a crime I didn't commit."

Donnie Grey smiled. The staged funeral had certainly taken a bit of planning. But he had his own reason for getting Tommy out of prison. He just hoped that the effort was worth it and he could now get some peace. He cursed the day he had confided his secret. He should have known that he could not trust Andy Spiers.

Jimmie looked across the table at Donnie. He was apprehensive when Donnie approached him five days earlier with the plan for the escape. He could not understand why Donnie was willing to help, as he had not seen Donnie for a number of years. But Donnie had reassured him that he was an old friend of Jimmie's father. Jimmie panicked at the word "coffin" in connection with the plan, but calmed down when Donnie stated that he did not actually have to go in the coffin, or get buried. Jimmie had then seen two points in favour of the plan. It would get his father out of prison and enable Jimmie to start a new life. He had been feeling for some time that he needed a change of lifestyle. He had been at a loose end for five years. Elsie Rooney's pregnancy had not helped matters.

Tommy stared into his empty mug. He found it difficult to fathom how the police had managed to convince themselves that the disappearance of Terry Thornton had anything to do with him. When Tommy was arrested, he had no idea, that the man in the Raigmore Tavern talking in a loud voice about "crooks" and "fiddles", was Terry Thornton. He knew that the man had some sort of official job, as he had seen him in the pub before with one of the local councillors. The only reason Tommy had threatened the man was because he had thought that the man was referring to his Hamish MacGregor pension scam, when he had mouthed off about "fiddles."

"Let's not forget the help that Ross MacKay gave us. We owe him a large drink" stated Donnie.

"Who the hell would have thought that Ross MacKay would have come to our rescue with a fake death certificate?" responded Jimmie. "Although let's be honest, the certificate would not have stood up to close scrutiny."

"There was very little likelihood of the prison authorities querying the certificate, particularly when handed in by a solicitor, although it was a stroke of luck they only provided one prison escort to the funeral."

"Ross MacKay and I knew each other in primary school over fifty years ago, but I didn't have us down as bosom buddies. I'm surprised he has gone to so much trouble," stated Tommy.

"Don't forget that Ross and I were cell mates in Inverness prison in the late sixties," Donnie commented.

"What about the van, will the police be looking for it?"

"No reason why they should. Peter Salah has been paid for it, so it won't be on a stolen vehicle report. Provided nobody saw us get in the van we should be fine."

"Right" said Jimmie, "let's get moving. With a bit of luck we should be in Chatham in a couple of hours. Let's hope your mate is happy to see us Donnie."

"Catch this. You're probably in need of a drink after your ordeal."

Tommy caught the hip flask thrown to him by Donnie. "You're right. I need something to get the taste of prison out of my mouth," he replied, unscrewing the cap.

CHAPTER FIFTY SIX

Inverness

Billy Saunders settled himself into his seat in the public bar of the Thistle Arms. He had just returned from the funeral wake for Jimmie Brown, a wake which had the appearance of going on for a further few days. It was a double celebration, the life of Jimmie Brown, and the escape of Tommy Brown.

Life was good for Billy. At the age of 62 he had a head of grey hair, but by maintaining a constant weight of fourteen stone for many years he was still an impressive figure of a man. Billy had a lust for life, and an inquisitive mind, which explains why he was sitting with a large brandy, and with a puzzled look on his face.

He had been at the graveside when Davie Brown collapsed, apparently overcome by grief at the death of his brother, and at the sight of his father in handcuffs. He had taken Davie to the nearby New Craigs Hospital, where it looked as though he would be in for a long stay. He had left the hospital when Davie started rambling about ghosts.

He had known Tommy Brown all his life. It was well known in the community that Tommy was a master at ducking and diving. If you wanted something, Tommy would find it for you.

Since his return to Inverness, Billy had seen Tommy on many occasions, and had exchanged a few words with him on each occasion. He recalled Tommy being at the wake for his father in the sixties.

Billy Saunders was prepared to stake his reputation that Tommy Brown was not a killer.

CHAPTER FIFTY SEVEN

Inverness

Sitting in the lounge bar of the Auld Lang Syne public house, fifty yards from the Thistle Arms, Alastair Winngate was romancing Elsie Rooney with tales of life in America. Elsie's consumption of gin and tonics was certainly not recommended for someone in her condition. But it had been a traumatic day. She had just buried her lover.

Elsie caressed her heavily pregnant stomach. She had to think of a name for the baby. She knew that it was to be a boy.

Earlier that day she had accompanied Billy Saunders when he had taken Davie Brown to the hospital. After hearing Davie ramble on about ghosts she decided that the Brown family were best forgotten.

But Alastair Winngate was a different kettle of fish. He was sophisticated and sexy. It didn't matter that he had a reputation with the girls. She could change him. And if she couldn't change him, did that really matter? Two can play around.

She quite liked the sound of "Elsie Winngate."

Elsie gripped Alastair's hand.

Another gin and tonic and she would have forgotten Jimmie Brown completely.

CHAPTER FIFTY EIGHT

Chatham

Charlie Fox, or Petty Cash as he now preferred to be called, looked at Willie Tosh, who was sitting opposite him in the Railway Inn, close to Chatham Station. The record of 72 year old Willie, from both a criminal and work perspective, had worsened as the years had passed. Willie had a reputation for completing work that was, not to put too fine a point on it, completely unsafe. And Willie was now sitting opposite Petty, seeking a favour.

"The source is reliable, as solid as houses," stated Willie, who was unaware of his own reputation for house building, and therefore missed the irony of his statement.

Petty frowned. He had been having a quiet drink when Willie entered the pub, clearly looking for somone. Willie's eyes had lit up when he saw Petty sitting on his own.

"There's a bloody good pay off for us if I get this work," continued Willie, rubbing his thumb and fingers together in the universal indication of a backhander.

"All right, I'll speak to Don Baxter. But no promises. If the inside information is correct about this development then, who knows, there might be a chance of a few grand each."

"I did some subcontracting work for the developer a couple of years ago. He owes me one, but I can't take the work in my own name. The Inland Revenue will take the bloody lot. As main contractor Don has the clout to allocate subbie work. My contact tells me that the developer and planner are as thick as thieves, and have exaggerated the scope of works. If Don gives you the work, I can carry out the work for you. We can inflate our quote without any fear of them saying too much. We could make a few grand out of this Petty."

Petty Cash looked out of the window. He wondered what he was letting himself in for. "If it's as sound as you say I'll see Don tonight. But I have to say that the re-surfacing of a municipal car park is hardly the project of the century."

"It's quite a big job, Petty. There's lots of excavation work before we can lay the new tarmac."

"I suppose you're right. I understand that the original contractor for the drainage system in the sixties made a botched job of it, and the foundations have sunk as a result. Whoever put in the car park on top of the drainage system years later should have noticed the problem."

Willie looked at Petty. He vividly remembered the original drainage and car park work. He had made a tidy profit on both jobs. "You'll not regret it," stated Willie.

Which, as a statement made in earnest, was greatly underestimating the powers of providence.

CHAPTER FIFTY NINE

Kent

It was late afternoon before the runaways pulled into Farthing Corner service station. They had arrived at the Chatham turn off a few minutes earlier, but seeing the low fuel level Donnie instructed Jimmie to drive direct to the service station.

"We'll get some petrol and a bite to eat. It'll give me a chance to phone the wife as well and let her know that I will be home this evening," commented Donnie.

"Thanks, I needed that," said Tommy, handing the hip flask to Donnie as he clambered out of the vehicle.

Tommy stumbled on the uneven forecourt. He grabbed at Donnie for support as he fell.

"Christ, how much have you had to drink? Is there any whisky left?"

"I've only taken a couple of sips. I'll make up for it this evening. A good whisky though."

"Glenfiddich. Only the best."

***

Twenty yards away, tucked behind the service station paying point, the driver of the police car nodded to himself. "I think that one may be worth having a word with, Todd. The old boy certainly looks drunk. It's a bloody pity he's not driving."

***

"How long have you known this mate of yours?" asked Jimmie.

"About forty years on and off. Petty Cash is a good mate.

He helped me when I returned to Chatham twenty years ago."

"That's a daft name isn't it? How the hell did he get a name like Petty Cash?"

"His real name is Charlie Fox. He's in his late fifties and a damn good builder."

"That doesn't explain the nickname."

"You wait until you see him. Petty Cash is the name he prefers to go by."

"I needed that coffee," commented Donnie, looking at his watch. "We'd better get a move on. Petty goes out drinking every evening. But first of all I've got to pay a visit to the gents."

"I'll go back to the van. I'll take over the driving for a while," remarked Tommy.

"Are you sure you feel up to it, Dad?"

"No problems, Jimmie. It'll wake me up."

Donnie and Jimmie made their way to the restroom whilst Tommy made his way back to the van. He was deep in thought.

Tommy sat in the driver's seat and brushed his fingers through his hair. He wondered how Davie was coping with the shock of attending his brother's funeral and seeing his father in handcuffs. It was a pity that Jimmie hadn't thought of contacting Davie in Spain, to tell him about the staged funeral escape plan. Davie had been a source of worry for some time. For someone unemployed he always had plenty of cash in his pocket. It had been that way for several years. But every time Tommy tackled him about how he had obtained the cash, Davie got angry. He had seemed even more uptight on the evening prior to his sudden trip to Spain.

Donnie and Jimmie watched the police car pull up alongside the transit van as they stepped out of the cafeteria.

Tommy, who had been leaning on the open window of the van, fell out of the van, when the door was pulled open.

"I was going to ask you to step out of the van, but you appear to have saved me the trouble."

Tommy looked at the police sergeant and constable

standing in front of him. He was puzzled. How the hell had the police got on to them so quickly?

"Can I see your driving licence?"

Tommy put his hand in his pocket, before he remembered that his driving licence and wallet were in the safe keeping of Irene Norman. "I don't have my licence with me," stated Tommy, acutely aware that there was a distinct smell of alcohol on his breath.

"Can you tell me the registration number of your vehicle?"

"I've no idea. I've borrowed the vehicle from a neighbour".

The sergeant looked at him. "We noticed you falling over. Have you been drinking?"

Tommy looked at the sergeant. "Just a small one"

"Get the breathalyser out of the car, Todd," the sergeant instructed the constable.

"Sorry sergeant. I forgot to put it in the car."

"Right, Todd. You drive the van down to the station, and search it when we get there. You," the sergeant continued, glaring at Tommy, "are coming to the station with me to be breathalysed. I don't know what your bloody game is but I'll find out."

Donnie and Jimmie watched the police car and van pull out of the service station.

"Let's get a taxi. It's a safe bet they're going to Rainham nick."

CHAPTER SIXTY

Chatham

Thirty minutes later Tommy was in an interview room at Rainham Police Station. Seated across a table from Tommy were Sergeant Bob Smithers and Constable Trevor Todd.

Tommy was relieved. The result of the breathalyser test taken minutes earlier had shown negative. But the police still had some questions for him.

The contents of Tommy's pocket lay on the table in front of him – a soiled handkerchief, a mobile phone, and a letter – the letter that Tommy had picked up from the hallway on his escape from his house.

The police sergeant picked up the letter. "Mr Hamish MacGregor, Inverness. You've come a long way haven't you, sir? What are you doing in this neck of the woods?"

Tommy pondered. How could he tell them that the previous day he had absconded from prison whilst attending his son's funeral, a son who was alive and well and in all probability sitting in a pub somewhere in the area of the police station.

"Right, if you are not prepared to answer that simple question, let's start at the beginning. I want your name and full address, date of birth, and occupation," the sergeant stated.

Tommy paused for a second. "Hamish MacGregor, 203 Craigton Avenue, Inverness. 20 May 1925, retired."

"How long have you lived at that address?"

"Over five years," replied Tommy, muttering a silent thank you to his over inquisitive postman who five years earlier had queried who Hamish MacGregor was, when pension statements had arrived at Tommy's house addressed to Hamish. He had asked Tommy some awkward questions at the time. Tommy had immediately contacted the local council and had Hamish's name put on the electoral roll. Seeing Hamish's name on the roll several weeks later had reassured the postman to the extent that he had even dropped in the odd book and magazine for the bedridden Hamish.

"What are you doing with the removal van?"

"I'm thinking of moving to Kent and am exploring the area," Tommy replied with a straight face. "It's been a long journey and I stopped at the service station for a coffee."

Sergeant Smithers had been making notes all the time the interview was taking place. "I'm just going to check one or two things."

The sergeant returned ten minutes later. "Your story seems to stack up. I've done a CRO check. There appears to be nothing against you. I've checked the van also. It is registered to a removal firm in Inverness. I've advised the Inverness police that you will report to them with your driving licence and insurance details within fourteen days."

Tommy left the police station and made his way to the transit van, which was parked in the police station car park. He breathed a sigh of relief as he manoeuvred the vehicle into Watling Street, and headed onto the busy Rainham High Street. He had no idea in which direction Chatham lay, but he had to get as far away as possible from the police station.

Meanwhile, back at the police station, Constable Todd was trying to explain why he had removed the suitcase from the transit van, and why he had not returned the suitcase to Mr MacGregor when he had left the police station.

Sergeant Smithers was only half listening. He was still contemplating how well Mr MacGregor looked for a man of seventy five.

CHAPTER SIXTY ONE

Twenty minutes after leaving the police station, Tommy Brown found himself in Faversham. By this time he had realised he was heading away from Chatham. Hoping that Jimmie had the sense to have his mobile phone switched on, Tommy dialled Jimmie's number. A very apprehensive Jimmie answered the call.

Fifteen minutes later Tommy picked up Donnie and Jimmie at the Cricketers public house in Rainham, two minutes walk from the police station. Donnie and Jimmie had made themselves comfortable in the public house. They had checked the police station car park after an hour, but seeing the transit van still there, had decided to lay low in the hope that Tommy rang them.

It was dark by the time they arrived in Chatham. They parked in a side street close to the railway station. Donnie pointed to a public house.

"There," he said, "the Chatham Arms pub, that's where Petty lives. He owns the pub."

Enquiries within the pub a minute later revealed that they had missed Petty. He was already on a pub crawl. It took two hours and three public houses before they made contact with him. They came across him in the Prince Albert standing next to the jukebox.

Tommy and Jimmie gazed at the figure standing in front of them. Petty Cash stood just over five foot tall. He was dressed all over in black leather, and wore cowboy boots. He was a mini version of Johnny Cash.

"I'll put you two up in the pub for tonight. We'll sort out permanent accommodation tomorrow," said Petty on their return to the Chatham Arms. "I expect Donnie will want to get home to his wife and kids."

Tommy opened the back of the van and realised that his

suitcase was missing. "The police have taken my suitcase. Well, they can bloody keep it. There's no way I'm going back to the police station."

Petty took the van keys from Tommy and handed them to one of the bar customers. "Take the van to Dover and leave it in the car park at the ferry terminal," he stated. He turned to Tommy and Jimmie. "With a bit of luck the police may think that you two have gone to France."

***

Two days after the incident at Rainham police station, the Northern Constabulary in Inverness were contacted by Kent Police, requesting that a visit be made to the home of Mr Hamish MacGregor to establish what he wanted done with the suitcase he had left in Rainham.

Later that day the Northern Constabulary reported back that there was nobody at Mr MacGregor's home. They added that they would check again the following day.

CHAPTER SIXTY TWO

Inverness

At the same time that the Kent Police were in communication with the Northern Constabulary about Hamish MacGregor, Billy Saunders was on the telephone to Sandy Burns at Inverness police station. Sandy and Billy had not been in touch with each other on an official basis since the investigation into the murders of Lorna Reid and Archie Stokes ten years earlier, although they had seen each other briefly at police social functions, and on the golf course.

"No developments on Lorna's murder then Sandy?"

"Not a thing. I'm afraid it may end up as one of those unsolved cases. We've also come to a halt on the Archie Stokes murder. Despite the discovery in Jackson's house of the items stolen from Stokes' house, I've never been convinced that Eddie Jackson had anything to do with the murder. Having discounted the piece of marble as the murder weapon, we searched Jackson's house after his funeral, looking for a possible weapon, but found nothing suspicious. It's possible that Jackson entered the house, executed the burglary and found Stokes' body. How his prints got on the piece of marble covered in Stokes' blood is a mystery. We have never been able to establish what it was that Lorna found out."

"After all this time, I'm not too optimistic we'll ever get the full picture. I've got another problem for you Sandy. This missing chap, Terence Thornton. I find it hard to believe that Tommy Brown has anything to do with his disappearance."

"You're not suggesting that Brown has been set up, in the same way that Jackson may have been? You don't think there's someone going around killing people, just to get some petty criminals in more serious trouble?"

Billy laughed. "I don't think it's quite that extreme. But there's definitely something odd going on."

CHAPTER SIXTY THREE

An hour after his arrival at Inverness police station Billy Saunders was introduced to the officer in charge of the investigation into the disappearance of Terry Thornton. Detective Inspector Ian Noble, who looked no older than mid-twenties, was clearly a fast track officer.

Ian Noble confirmed that Tommy Brown was the only suspect in what was almost certainly a murder enquiry. Following Tommy's escape from prison via the cemetery the police visited his house and found a blood stained knife. Medical records confirmed that the blood group on the knife was the same blood group as Terry Thornton's. There were only two sets of fingerprints on the knife, Terry Thornton's and Tommy Brown's. The knife was being treated as a possible murder weapon.

"The irony of the situation," stated Ian, "is that just prior to Brown's escape we were having serious doubts as to whether a murder had been committed. It is highly likely that he would have been released from custody within days. Without a body, or even a crime scene, it is difficult for us to prove that a murder has been committed. But finding the fingerprints on the blood stained knife, along with the blood stained jacket, has changed our view. We now believe that Thornton has been murdered, and that Brown is responsible. We have no leads on where Brown disappeared to, or who his escape accomplice was. We have found the hearse but the driver wore gloves. Statements have been taken from all those attending the funeral. None of the mourners knew who the pallbearer was. Which is total crap of course, every one in the district probably knows who he is."

"Does it not seem odd to you that a bloodstained knife should be conveniently found in Tommy Brown's house so long after Thornton's disappearance?"

"Not really. At the time of the murder Brown was shacking up with his girl friend Irene Norman. When we visited her place and found the bloodstained jacket we saw no point in checking Brown's home. The knife has obviously been there all this time."

Billy Saunders left the police station ten minutes later.

Tommy Brown was no fool. Had Tommy murdered Terry Thornton, there was no way that he would have left the murder weapon in his house. He was even more convinced that Tommy Brown was innocent.

Something was not quite right.

CHAPTER SIXTY FOUR

Chatham

Tommy Brown was frustrated. He was normally a fastidious dresser, even though his taste in clothing was inappropriate for his age. Following the loss of the suitcase containing the clothes that Jimmie had packed for him, he spoke to Donnie Grey and advised him that he needed money.

"This should cover any eventuality," Donnie stated, handing Tommy a large envelope. "Passports, driving licences, credit cards, new bank accounts, and some money. None of the documents are in your real name. You have to keep your head down for a while, Tommy. In a week or so, once they have stopped checking the ports, you can both disappear altogether."

"I don't know how we can ever repay you, or Ross MacKay."

Donnie shrugged. "You'd have done the same for me. You can pay me back one day. However, I have to rush as I am going to Brighton for a couple of days. I'll see you when I get back."

***

Tommy looked at his new identity papers bearing the name Paul Norman. They certainly looked authentic. He wondered where Ross MacKay had got the passport photograph from. Tommy looked five years younger in the photograph, but this tied in with the date of issue of the passport. With the fake driving licence, credit cards, and new bank account, he had a whole new identity. Donnie Grey had gone to great lengths to get him out of prison, and prepare him for a life on the run. He assumed that Paul Norman had been a real person. No doubt someone who had died in infancy had his identity stolen. Jimmie's papers bore the name David Young.

Tommy wondered why Donnie Grey and Ross MacKay were going to so much trouble. He had asked Donnie on several occasions why he was helping but had not received a clear cut answer. Tommy was intrigued. Whilst he was grateful to be out of prison, he wondered what was really going on in the background. Tommy was not used to hand-outs, apart from those extracted from the social security. He had an uncomfortable feeling that he was a pawn in a much bigger game.

CHAPTER SIXTY FIVE

Two days after Inverness Police received the phone call from Rainham about Hamish Macgregor's suitcase they contacted Rainham to advise them that there was no sign of Mr MacGregor at the Craigton Avenue address. The Scottish police pointed out however, that the registered tenant of the house in question was Thomas Brown, an escaped prisoner.

Sergeant Smithers decided to open the suitcase. The suitcase contained soiled clothing, four hundred king size cigarettes, and a toilet bag.

It took Sergeant Smithers ten minutes to discover the false lining in the suitcase. In the false lining he found a large quantity of used Spanish and Sterling bank notes. On checking the conversion rate for the peseta, Sergeant Smithers was astounded to discover that the find amounted to two hundred and forty thousand pounds.

Detective Chief Inspector Ted Williams was informed.

Kent County Constabulary issued an all stations bulletin stating that Thomas Brown should be apprehended on sight.

CHAPTER SIXTY SIX

Chatham

Billy Saunders had just stepped out of the shower when he received a call from Ian Noble advising him that there was a development in the hunt for Tommy Brown. Ian advised Billy that the Kent police were certain, that Tommy Brown had turned up in Kent with a suitcase full of money. With time on his hands, Billy decided to play a more active part in the investigation.

Billy arrived in Chatham the following afternoon, and booked into the Bridgewood Manor Hotel. Before leaving Inverness he asked Ian Noble to contact Chatham police to alert them to his arrival on the scene. The last thing he wanted to do was to tread on toes.

He need not have worried, as the moment he arrived at Chatham Police Station, he was greeted by Chief Inspector Ted Williams.

"Good to see you again Billy. I heard that you had retired. Just can't keep away from it can you?"

"You're a fine one to talk. You must be quite a few years over retirement age. Haven't the force had enough of you yet?"

"You know the problems. You try to retire and they talk you out of it. But I've decided that I'll retire next year. I'm not getting any younger, and the force has changed quite a bit since you and I were young officers. There is too much interference from the Home Office and this bloody government."

"I'll go along with that. I made the right move when I retired and went back to my roots. I bought a few pubs in Inverness. It's a different type of life but I enjoy it."

It took Ted Williams ten minutes to outline the incident

involving Tommy Brown, the suitcase, and the money.

"And the name on the van – Salah?"

"That's it. Mean anything to you?"

"There's a small removal firm in Inverness by that name. We could check with them, but I suspect we will be told that the van has been nicked. Still, it's a starting point."

"I'm sure we'll solve the mystery in the end."

"Have there been any developments on your unsolved murders? Or is that a daft question? I dare say you've had another dozen murders in your area since we last met."

"More than a dozen I'm afraid, Billy. But fortunately most of them have been solved. There are a couple of interesting ones, however. Two doctors murdered, each strangled with a necktie. The same MO as the Ann Stanton investigation you were involved in during the early eighties."

"We never did solve those murders. But it's not my problem now. How's Christine by the way?"

"She's fine. I'll tell her you are here. No doubt she will want to see you."

"I'll see how time goes, Ted. I may only be here a day or two."

CHAPTER SIXTY SEVEN

Chatham

Billy Saunders had been in Chatham only twenty four hours when he ran into Tommy Brown. Tommy was hardly disguising himself, or hiding away. He walked out of the door of a flat in Chatham High Street, a flat provided by Petty Cash, at the same moment as Billy exited the nearby Nat West bank.

Tommy was moving at a fast pace and Billy had to step out to keep up with him. Judging by the street signs Tommy was heading in the direction of the railway station.

Billy checked his watch. It was just after midday. He had arranged to play golf with Ted Williams that afternoon. He flipped open his mobile. Ted would have to wait.

Tommy walked past Chatham railway station, and then veered left. He walked for about four hundred yards, through streets of old terraced houses. Billy followed at a discreet distance. The area was quiet. If Tommy turned around he would almost certainly see him.

Billy turned the corner into the street that Tommy had just entered. There was no sign of Tommy. Billy looked around. The only building in the street, apart from terraced houses, was the Chatham Arms. Tommy could have entered any one of the houses, or the public house. "Sod it" muttered Billy.

Despite the early hour the public house was packed. Billy edged his way to the bar and looked at the pumps. "A pint of best bitter and a packet of salt and vinegar."

Billy looked into the mirror behind the bar. There was no sign of Tommy at the bar. It looked as though he had gone into one of the terraced houses.

A couple of men wearing overalls moved away from the

bar, allowing Billy to see into the bar seating area.

He nearly dropped his glass.

Only thirty years of police discipline enabled him to hold onto his drink.

Sitting in the bar was Jimmie Brown. The same Jimmie Brown whose funeral he had attended four days previously. Sitting next to him was Tommy Brown.

Billy continued to stare into the mirror. A broad grin crossed his face. He walked over to the Browns, who were in deep conversation. "Well, I'll say this much for you two. You pulled a bloody good stunt."

Tommy Brown looked up. It took him a few seconds to realise who it was. "Billy. What the hell are you doing down here?"

"Looking for you. Although I must admit I did not expect to wake the dead at the same time."

Jimmie began to rise.

"Sit down Jimmie. I'm not here to cause problems. But after seeing you two together, I must admit that a large malt would go down well."

***

"Right, Tommy. Fill me in. How was the escape organised? Is Terry Thornton dead? Where did the money come from?"

"Money, what money?" asked Tommy. "I don't know anything about any money, and I haven't a clue where Terry Thornton is."

"OK. I've got all day. Tell me what you *do* know."

It took fifteen minutes for Tommy to brief Billy about the escape.

"Who the hell is Donnie Grey?"

"An old neighbour from the seventies. He used to lodge next door to us in Inverness."

"Let me get this straight. A neighbour, who you haven't seen for over twenty years, suddenly turns up and helps you to escape from prison. Doesn't that strike you as odd?"

"I suppose so," said Tommy. "But put yourself in my shoes. I'm in the nick for something I didn't do, with the possibility of a life sentence. Somebody offers to get me out. Am I supposed to ask for references?"

"I take your point, but it does seem odd. What does this Donnie Grey look like?"

"A right ugly bastard. He's got a scar running down the side of his face. He's about sixty, grey haired, just over six feet, on the heavy side."

"Right, I'll make enquiries at Chatham nick. In the meantime I suggest you two keep your heads down. The police are looking for you Tommy."

Billy was at the door of the pub before he realised that he had not asked any questions about the suitcase. "Where did you get the case from?"

"It must have been the one Davie brought back from his holiday. I just picked it up from the hallway, thinking it was the one that Jimmie had packed my clothes in," replied Tommy.

"Talking about Davie reminds me. He collapsed at the cemetery and is in New Craigs Hospital. It's not life threatening. I'll make enquiries as to how he is, and I'll see you back here tomorrow evening. Say eight o'clock."

Billy walked out of the pub without waiting for a response.

CHAPTER SIXTY EIGHT

Chatham

Shortly after Billy Saunders left the Chatham Arms, Donnie Grey arrived back from Brighton. He joined Tommy and Jimmie for a drink.

"We've got a visitor from Inverness."

"Who?"

"Billy Saunders, he owns several pubs. He used to be with the London police. I'm afraid that he saw Jimmie and I."

Donnie looked at Tommy. "Any idea what he wants?"

"He's looking into the disappearance of Terry Thornton, also something about a case full of money."

"Money, what money?"

"That's exactly what I said to him. Anyway, how was Brighton?"

"It was fine," replied Donnie, deep in thought.

"So you start work with Willie Tosh tomorrow?" commented Donnie, looking at Jimmie.

"Yeah. I had a word with Willie about a job. Seven o'clock start at the municipal car park at the riverside in Chatham."

Donnie Grey stared at Jimmie. "What does the job entail?"

"As far as I know we are digging up a car park and re-surfacing it. Willie reckons that there is ten days work because of some drainage problems. There's a pub a few yards away from the site."

"The Command House?"

"Aye, that's it."

Donnie Grey looked thoughtful. "I might visit the site myself tomorrow. I'm supposed to be working at Gillingham Football Club on the new stadium, but Petty Cash has asked me to keep an eye on what Willie Tosh gets up to. I'll see you in the morning. I'm going to stay here for another drink."

"What's bugging Donnie?" asked Jimmie when they were out of earshot.

"No idea. But something happened in the last couple of days to upset him."

CHAPTER SIXTY NINE

Chatham

The work on digging up the municipal car-park had been underway three hours when Willie Tosh called a halt. The driver of a small digger was waving frantically at Willie.

"For Christ sake what's the problem Jerry? We're strapped for time on this job."

"I think we've got a problem, take a look at this," said Jerry Moore, pointing to a white object lying in the deep hole he had dug.

Willie Tosh clambered into the hole, and worked his way under the redundant drainage pipes. "Mother of God," he exclaimed. "It's a skull, and a human one at that. Switch off the digger Jerry." Willie climbed out of the hole, clutching the skull in his hands.

Donnie Grey and Jimmie Brown looked at the skull.

"Contact the police Donnie, and while you are at it, you'd better let Petty know as well."

Four hours later a police forensic team unearthed the remains of two bodies. The remnants of a naval uniform clung to the bones of one of the skeletons. A Timex watch hung loosely on the wrist bone of the second skeleton.

"I want all work suspended on this site until further notice," stated a uniformed police inspector. "A detailed forensic search will have to be made of the whole area. There may well be other bodies."

Petty Cash, who had arrived on the scene only ten minutes earlier, having travelled from a job in north London, pulled Willie Tosh to one side. "Remind me Willie. What was our deal with Don Baxter?"

"We gave him ten grand up front for the contract. We get paid fifty five grand on completion of the job. That gives us twenty grand clear profit."

"Completion date?"

"The job has to be completed in ten days."

"Penalty clauses?"

"Five grand a day after the ten days."

Petty walked across to the senior police officer.

"Any idea when we can restart work?"

The officer looked at him. "With the size of this site you'll be lucky to re-start work within two weeks. Forensics will have to do an inch by inch search, until I am satisfied that the whole area is clear."

Petty Cash turned around.

Willie Tosh was nowhere to be seen.

"Why?" moaned Petty. "Why do I fall for Willie Tosh's "sure things" every time? If there hadn't been skeletons, it probably would have been the site of the Black Death or something else. I'll kill the little bugger."

CHAPTER SEVENTY

Chatham

With work for the day being abandoned, Tommy and Jimmie visited the Chatham Arms. A check of the Dover ferry terminal car park had revealed that the area around Salah's van was sealed off with police tape. As there was now a reasonable chance that the police believed that Tommy was on the continent, there was less likelihood that anyone would be looking for them in the Chatham area.

Billy Saunders walked into the public house at eight o'clock.

Jimmie walked to the bar.

"What can I get you, Billy?"

"I'm fine for the moment, but I need to talk to you and Tommy in private. Is there anywhere we can go?"

"There's a sitting room upstairs. I'm sure that Petty won't mind us using it for a few minutes."

Seated in the comfortable lounge in Petty Cash's living area, Billy got straight to the point. "There's no easy way to say this I'm afraid. I spoke to Inverness police this morning. Davie is dead."

"Dead, what do you mean dead?" said Jimmie.

"Murdered. He discharged himself from hospital yesterday evening. His body was found in an alley off Church Street late last night. The murderer was disturbed in the act, but got away."

Tommy sunk his head in his hands.

"Did Davie have any enemies?"

"Nobody we are aware of."

Jimmie put his arm around Tommy.

"I asked Inverness police the same question. They checked their old records. Davie's name cropped up in a couple of incidents in the eighties. It appears that he was threatened by someone named Danny Forsyth twenty years ago. Forsyth was sentenced to ten years imprisonment at the time. According to the Inverness police, Forsyth was arrested on a drunk and disorderly charge in Inverness only last week."

"Of even more interest," Billy continued, "is the fact that Donnie Grey was cautioned in the eighties for threatening Davie. It appears that there was a disagreement in an Inverness pub, and Grey threatened to kill Davie if he ever saw him again. It's curious that Chatham police have no record against Donnie Grey in the sixties, nor since his return to Chatham in the eighties, yet in Inverness he has a record of violence. What happened in Scotland to change him?"

"None of this makes sense," said Tommy.

"I agree. But there is a link somewhere between Davie and Donnie Grey. Is Donnie around?"

"He got back from Brighton yesterday evening."

"What was he doing in Brighton?"

"No idea."

Billy looked thoughtful,

"I think we'd better have a word with him."

"I'll leave that to you and Jimmie. I'm going back to Inverness to give myself up. I want to see Davie's body," said Tommy.

Billy nodded. "It's probably the most sensible thing to do."

CHAPTER SEVENTY ONE

Chatham

The following morning Tommy Brown was driven to Gatwick Airport, where he caught the one hour flight to Inverness. Billy Saunders had telephoned Ian Noble from the airport to advise him that Tommy was giving himself up. Tommy was picked up by a police car at Inverness Airport, and was taken straight to the police mortuary. An hour later he was back in Porterfield Prison.

Billy Saunders and Jimmie Brown sat in the departure lounge at Gatwick.

"Another coffee?"

Jimmie shook his head.

"As I see it Jimmie, we have a number of issues to sort out. We have to figure out who killed Davie, and why. We also need to find out where Terry Thornton is. Is he alive or dead? How did your father's fingerprints get on a blood stained knife handled by Terry Thornton? What is the significance of the money in the case? And finally, what connection has Donnie Grey with all of this? One thing is for sure. Donnie Grey is involved somehow."

CHAPTER SEVENTY TWO

Gillingham

Billy Saunders and Jimmie Brown tracked down Donnie Grey in the Prince Albert public house. Donnie was sitting at a corner table. He looked the worse for wear.

"Can I get you a drink Donnie?"

Donnie Grey looked up. "Leave me alone. I just want some peace and quiet."

Ignoring Donnie's request, Billy sat down, whilst Jimmie went to the bar. "We need to talk. I have the feeling that you know a great deal more than you are letting on."

"Sod off. I've got nothing to say to you," Donnie slurred.

"Just a few questions, then I'm out of your hair."

Jimmie placed a drink in front of Billy.

"Why did you go to such great lengths to get Tommy out of prison?"

Donnie held his head in his hands.

"All right Donnie, if you're not prepared to answer that question, here's another. Is Terry Thornton alive or dead?"

"I've no bloody idea. I don't know the man."

Billy picked up his drink. "Do you know anything about Davie's murder?"

"No. But I had reason to kill him. He's the one that gave me this scar," Donnie replied, touching his face.

"What about the money? Any idea where that came from?"

"You're wasting your time, I can't tell you anything. If I do, my family may get hurt."

Donnie Grey stood up. His mouth was twitching, and his eyes flickering.

Billy was startled to see the frightened look on Donnie's face.

"I'm leaving now. I need to think some things through."

Donnie Grey staggered out of the public house. The light from the telephone box caught his eye. He dialled a number. "It's me. I have to see you. The Scottish copper is asking questions."

Donnie listened to the reply.

"All right, I'll see you at the dockyard tomorrow afternoon."

CHAPTER SEVENTY THREE

Chatham

The object looked like a bundle of rags to ten year old James York. He had been at Chatham Historic Dockyard only twenty minutes, but already the signs of boredom had set in. This was no reflection on the dockyard attractions. It was a reflection on the state of mind of most of the ten year olds who were on the school trip organised by Chatham Boys School, a school trip that had already driven one of the escorting teachers to tears.

He had been walking up and down outside the Ropery exhibition for five minutes before he saw the bundle.

James looked at the object on the ground. He pulled his foot back to take a kick at it, then paused. He looked again. He was sure that he must be mistaken.

He drew in his breath as he realised what he was looking at. A face, a face contorted in anguish. A face that was very clearly dead.

James ran into the Ropery, shouting at the top of his voice, "Miss, Miss, you'd better come and see this."

Mrs Joyce Green, decades after actually being a Miss, suddenly found herself in the grasp of a ten year old child who was babbling incoherently. But she got the general idea of what young James wanted, when he kicked her in order to get her attention.

One minute later the relative quiet of Chatham Historic Dockyard was shattered by screams from Mrs Green

Sergeant Bob Smithers and Constable Trevor Todd were on patrol in the Brompton area of Chatham when the call came over the radio alerting them to a disturbance in the dockyard.

They reached the dockyard in two minutes.

A minute later the patrol car was parked outside the Ropery.

Sergeant Smithers gazed at the body of a large man. He looked up as the senior officer approached.

"How does it look to you, sergeant? Suicide?"

"Bit early to say boss, but my money is on either an accident or suicide. The kid over there reckons he saw the man jump from the fourth floor."

CHAPTER SEVENTY FOUR

Chatham

Extract from the Chatham Gazette dated 20th November 2000

MAN DIES IN DOCKYARD FALL

The body of sixty year old Rainham man Donald Arnold Grey was found in Chatham Historic Dockyard yesterday. According to a police spokesman Mr Grey had fallen from a fourth floor window of an old storeroom.

Unconfirmed reports state that the fall was witnessed by a ten year schoolboy who was visiting the dockyard with a school party.

The police are speculating that Mr Grey was visiting the dockyard as he had worked there in the sixties, in the very building from which he fell. He is survived by his widow Mrs Shona Grey, and two children.

The Gazette understands that Mrs Grey has stated that her husband has been depressed for some time. The police say that there are no suspicious circumstances relating to the incident.

An inquest is to be held.

Billy Saunders read the report whilst having breakfast. With a puzzled look on his face he tore the article from the newspaper and placed it in his wallet.

CHAPTER SEVENTY FIVE

Chatham

"I don't know what the hell is going on, but I intend to find out. The police report states that Donnie's death could have been an accident or suicide. The police arrived on the scene within a few minutes and checked the area immediately. There was no indication that any other person had been with Donnie at the time of his death. According to a ten year old kid, who reckons he saw the whole thing, Donnie jumped from a fourth floor window. Given the state of Donnie when we saw him yesterday, I suppose that's possible. But we still need to establish who had been threatening him. Inverness appears to be the starting point. Was Donnie involved in Davie's death? He could have been, if he went to Inverness instead of Brighton. But if he *did* kill Davie, why? We'll check with Donnie's wife to find out if she knew who he is supposed to have visited in Brighton."

Jimmie picked up his coffee, and looked at the snack menu on the table. He caught the eye of the passing waiter. "Don't know about you Billy but I'm starving. Do you want something to eat?"

"You go ahead. Get me a sandwich of some kind. I'm going up to my room to make a couple of calls."

Jimmie glanced around the lounge area. The Bridgewood Manor Hotel was certainly classy. He could quite easily enjoy the lifestyle.

Billy returned after thirty minutes. He sat down, and glanced at the empty plate.

"Sorry Billy, I was hungrier that I realised. I'll order some more sandwiches."

"No time. I've just been speaking to the Chatham police. Ted Williams wasn't there, but I got a lot of help from a

Sergeant Rogers. Rogers was a probationary copper in Chatham in the sixties. He's expecting us in a couple of hours. But before that we are going to visit Shona Grey."

CHAPTER SEVENTY SIX

Chatham

It was evident that Donnie Grey had been proud of his home. The beautiful garden attested to that.

Billy Saunders and Jimmie Brown approached the house warily. Billy had visited too many bereaved relatives in his career. Jimmie's mind was in turmoil, thinking of Davie. He'd had enough personal grief. He had no need to share in the grief of Shona Grey.

Shona Grey opened the door before they knocked. The signs of grief were evident on her face. "Thank you for seeing us Mrs Grey. It is important; otherwise we would not have troubled you."

"Sit down whilst I put the kettle on. Tea or coffee?"

***

Billy placed the coffee cup on the table. He and Jimmie had been with Shona Grey for half an hour, talking about Donnie and his lifestyle.

"Just a couple of more questions, if I may? Did Donnie have any enemies as far as you know?"

"None, apart from a man named MacInver. Donnie broke down one evening and confided to me what MacInver did to him in prison many years ago. Donnie was afraid that MacInver would come after him when he got out of prison. Donnie was a very loving family man. He doted on the two children, although they're not children any more," she said, glancing at a photograph on the coffee table. "James is at university. Susan is married, and has a young daughter."

"How had Donnie been lately? Had he seemed worried, depressed?"

"Yes. He had been preoccupied since his recent visit to Inverness. He went there to help a friend. It's also a bad time of year because of what happened to his parents and his sister. I had no idea that he felt suicidal."

"This friend in Inverness, have you any idea who it is?"

"I'm not sure. He got a call at home one evening and became very agitated with the caller. The following day he had a further call, as a result of which he said, he was going to Inverness straight away. Whatever he was asked to do obviously bothered him, but it was as though he had no choice. I reminded him that James was due home from university, but he still went to Inverness.

"You mentioned that Donnie had a sister. Tell me about her."

"She lived in Chatham until the early sixties. She moved to Brighton when her boyfriend ditched her. Her mother and father drove her down to Brighton at the time. There was an accident on the way and Donnie's parents died in the crash. His sister survived, but she has been in a mental hospital ever since. He visited her every year on the anniversary of the accident. The only time he'd missed an annual visit was when he was in prison."

"So Donnie visited Brighton last week to see her."

Shona Grey nodded. "He came back depressed. I think the visit may have been what tipped him over the edge. Although I find it hard to believe that he committed suicide. He adored his family." She sobbed softly.

"One final question. Was there anyone from his past in the Medway towns that he was still in touch with?"

"Not as far as I am aware."

"I think we've taken up enough of your time Mrs Grey. I'll give you my mobile phone number. If there is anything that Jimmie and I can do to help please don't hesitate to call."

"There is one thing Mr Saunders. I don't know if it is important. The calls from Inverness. The first caller was a woman."

"A woman?"

"Yes. She said her name was Sheila Jennison speaking on behalf of some firm, Highland something or other, I can't remember the full name. She asked to speak to Donnie. I seem to recall Donnie lodging with a Sheila Jennison many years ago in Inverness."

***

Billy wound down the car window.

"I wonder what Sheila Jennison wanted?"

"The last I heard she was still locked up in a mental home. She's not been seen in Inverness for years."

"Perhaps she has been released under care in the community nonsense, probably drugged up to the eyeballs. I wonder if she is dangerous. I hope they haven't released a potential killer."

"Let's not forget this MacInver guy. We'll have to find out who he is and what he is up to."

CHAPTER SEVENTY SEVEN

Chatham

Sergeant Rowland Rogers, or Roy as he was known within the force, certainly looked as though he had been around in the sixties. He was much the same age as Billy Saunders, but the desk job had clearly taken its toll. Standing at five foot nine inches and grey haired, Roy Rogers weighed in at seventeen stone.

"The chief super has been on at me for years to lose weight. But every time the opportunity came up for me to get a beat job he insisted that I continue looking after the paperwork. Local knowledge, that's my problem. Born in Chatham and certain to die in Chatham. Not a thing has happened in the Medway towns in the past fifty years that I don't know about. So how can I help?"

"You mentioned on the phone that you remembered Donnie Grey and his associates from the sixties, prior to his moving out of the area. Fill me in."

"Donnie Grey, a real charmer with the ladies. A classy dresser. When not at work he was always in teddy boy gear. He bummed around with a few of the local lads. There was talk about Grey being involved in drugs with a bloke called Andy Spiers and another couple of hoodlums, but nothing was ever proven. Spiers was a right hard nut, always wandering around in his work clothes. There is no record of any charges against either of them, which is surprising. They both left the area in, I would guess, the mid sixties. I've no idea where Grey went to, although he came back to Medway in the early eighties. We've never had any problems with him since his return. A great pity, the way he died. He must have had a lot on his mind to commit suicide. Andy Spiers went to London with his fancy piece. The Met Police got in touch with us, probably early to mid-eighties, looking for Spiers' woman."

"What type of work did Grey do in the sixties?"

"He was a storeman at the dockyard as I recall. Half the town worked there. It was the death of Chatham when the navy left and the dockyard closed. The daft thing is the town was a damn sight safer in those days. We had a saying then that no respectable woman would walk down the Brook after six in the evening, being as it was the haunt of the prossies."

Billy interrupted the sergeant in mid flow. "These mates of Donnie Grey. You said that one of them, Andy Spiers, was a hard nut. Tell me about him."

"He was known to walk around with knuckle dusters, and even a knife at times. Nowadays it's guns. What the hell is happening to the world?"

Billy once again interrupted the sergeant. "What was Spiers full name? I knew someone called Spiers in the sixties."

"I never had the chance to find out. He was never booked for anything."

"You mentioned that Spiers always wore his work clothes. What exactly did he do for a living?"

"That's an easy one for me to remember because of my grandfather. He…"

Billy held up his hand. "Grandfather? What about your grandfather?"

"I was just telling you. Andy Spiers helped lay him to rest."

"Lay him to rest?" queried Jimmie.

"Bury him. Andy Spiers worked in a funeral parlour."

CHAPTER SEVENTY EIGHT

Chatham

"I'm drowning in this stuff," stated Jimmie, gazing at the cup of coffee he held in his hands.

"We need clear heads Jimmie. I'm desperate for a pint as well, but I feel we are very close to solving part of the puzzle."

Billy and Jimmie were back in the hotel, discussing the information they had just received from Sergeant Rogers.

"We need to go right back to the beginning. Only someone with money and contacts could have carried out the elaborate escape plan. Who paid for the funeral? Who provided the hearse? Who liaised with the cemetery authorities? It's too much of a coincidence that Donnie Grey's best mate in the sixties was an undertaker. We need to find out what happened to Andy Spiers. Has he ever been to Inverness?"

"I've not heard that name mentioned in Inverness and I've lived there for forty years."

Billy looked at Jimmie. "How many funeral parlours are there in Inverness?"

"No idea. I'd say probably about half a dozen."

"How many of these employ men in their late fifties, early sixties."

"No idea."

"Well there can't be that many. I'm going to give Ian Noble a call. Ian can find out for us, and with a bit of luck he may be able to get photographs of those who fit the bill."

Two hours later the receptionist at the Bridgewood Manor advised Billy that an email had arrived for him. The email and scanned photographs were from Ian Noble. Only two funeral directors fitted the age criteria.

"Donald Gregory. Gregory and MacPherson Undertakers. I know them well enough. They buried my dad in the sixties. Donald Gregory is probably the most well known and respected undertaker in the Highlands. His father and grandfather ran the business before him. I can't think there would be anything odd with him."

Billy Saunders picked up the second photograph. He glanced at the details.

"Robbie Stephens, the Highland Funeral Parlour. It says here he opened the business in 1982. Mean anything to you?"

"The Highland Funeral Parlour! That's the company who staged the funeral allowing Dad to escape. I've seen ads in the Courier about their services. Can't say I've ever met Robbie Stephens though, or heard anything untoward about him. I think he's involved in some charity work, and the local council."

"Robbie Stephens. I've heard that name before. I just can't think what it's in connection with. Let's visit Sergeant Rogers and see if he can help."

CHAPTER SEVENTY NINE

Roy Rogers looked at the photograph of Donald Gregory and shook his head. "I can't say he bears a resemblance to any of our old villains."

Billy passed him the photograph of Robbie Stephens.

Roy Rogers stared at it for a few seconds.

"Give me a minute. I just want to check something out." It was five minutes before he returned. He was accompanied by an even older looking sergeant. "Eric has been at the station as long as I have. He confirms what I thought."

Billy waited expectantly.

"The man in the photograph has aged quite a bit, but I am almost certain he is Andy Spiers. Eric is equally convinced that the woman next to him is Ann Stanton, Spier's girl-friend in the sixties. But we are curious as to where the photograph was taken. It looks like an official police function."

Billy Saunders glanced at the email in his hand.

"Spot on. The photo was taken at a police awards ceremony."

"I can't imagine what these two would be doing at a police awards ceremony. These two are pure evil, as bad as the moors murderers. If you're looking for suspects, look no further. Incidentally, since I last saw you I've had a chance to check the register of births. Spiers' full name is Andrew Robert Spiers. He had a younger sister, but she died years ago."

"Are you quite sure about the relationship between Spiers and Ann Stanton?"

"Absolutely, they were inseparable."

Billy Saunders grimaced.

"Remind me where Robbie Stephens' funeral parlour is in Inverness, Jimmie."

"In Church Street, the back of the parlour leads onto the alley where Davie was murdered."

Billy looked at the photograph again. "I've seen her before. When I took Lorna Reid to a Police Ball in Inverness some years ago this woman was sitting at the next table. It's strange, I thought at the time she looked vaguely familiar. I must have seen a photograph of her at some time. I know the name Ann Stanton well. But this is the first time I have heard her linked to Andy Spiers, which I find quite surprising."

"What do you mean, surprising?"

"Oh, just passing thoughts Jimmie."

***

When Billy Saunders contacted Ian Noble later that day, one further piece of information came to light. The clerk at Inverness police station, who had assisted Ian Noble in the search for a photograph of the two undertakers, recalled speaking to one of the undertakers in the Ness Hotel bar ten days earlier. The subject of conversation had been the imminent release of Tommy Brown. The name of the undertaker was Robbie Stephens.

CHAPTER EIGHTY

Inverness

The following morning Billy Saunders and Jimmie Brown took the early morning flight from Gatwick to Inverness. Billy had phoned Ian Noble the previous evening explaining that he needed to see him as a matter of urgency, but the meeting had to be held in Billy's flat, not at the police station.

Ian arrived at the flat one hour after Billy and Jimmie's arrival in Inverness. "What's so important?"

"There's someone here you need to meet," said Billy.

Jimmie stepped out of the kitchen.

"Meet the late departed James Brown, who to all intents and purposes is six feet under in Tomnahurich cemetery."

Jimmie held out his hand.

"You'd better fill me in," said Ian Noble, sitting down.

***

"This is a lot to take in. The Stephens have a good reputation in the town. I met them at the recent police awards ceremony. They are a major part of the business community. Mrs Stephens is treasurer of the Ladies Institute and Robbie Stephens is a member of the Round Table. You are quite sure about this Spiers and Stanton business?"

"One hundred per cent. But there's no crime in changing your name. I've asked the Met Police to dig around to see if the name Andy Spiers appears on any old records. I know the name Ann Stanton will surface. In the meantime I think we ought to pay Stephens a visit."

Ian Noble nodded in agreement.

"But Jimmie stays in the flat. As far as the world is concerned he is dead, and he'll remain that way until we find out why Stephens has supposed to have buried him."

"Agreed, and at this stage Stephens is not to be made aware that we know who he really is."

CHAPTER EIGHTY ONE

Billy Saunders placed his coffee cup on the table and looked around the reception area at The Highland Funeral Parlour. He and Ian Noble had arrived there fifteen minutes earlier. An attentive receptionist had welcomed them on their arrival at the funeral home. She was taken aback when Ian Noble explained that they wished to see Robbie Stephens on official police business, rather than on a bereavement matter.

Billy stretched his legs. The visitors' chairs had clearly been designed for appearance rather than comfort.

"Strange places funeral parlours. It strikes me as an odd occupation, dealing with death every day. I've never felt comfortable giving bad news. One part of the job I don't miss."

He picked up a coloured brochure and thumbed through it. "The price of some of these coffins is astronomical."

Ian was saved from replying when the receptionist spoke.

"Mr Stephens is ready to see you now gentlemen."

Ian was at the door to Robbie Stephen's office before he realised that Billy had not moved from the funereal display area in the centre of the reception area.

"Billy?"

"Coming, I was miles away," replied Billy, tearing himself away from the items in the display case.

Ian made the introductions between Robbie Stephens and Billy.

"I assume this is a social call, gentlemen," commented Robbie Stephens. "You are both looking far too well to need my business services."

"It's official police business I'm afraid. We are here to talk about a funeral you arranged just over a week ago, James Brown from Craigton Avenue. Ring any bells?"

"I remember it well."

"Was there anything odd about the funeral, Robbie?"

"Odd? What do you mean odd?"

"The fact that Mr Brown was not dead will do for starters."

Robbie Stephens looked at both men. "Ah! Well, I suppose it was too much to expect that we could get away with it."

"Get away with what precisely?"

Robbie Stephens stood up. He removed his spectacles, and wiped them on the front of his shirt. "I was with the usual crowd at the golf club nine or ten days ago. The talk got around to Tommy Brown being in prison for a crime he had not committed. Too many innocent people get locked away for a long time. I have known the Brown family for many years, and I felt that something had to be done to help Tommy. I understood that there was little chance of parole before a trial, and as far as the police were concerned, Tommy was already judged guilty. I decided to assist in his escape. A few of us concocted the fake funeral idea to get him out of prison."

"You do realise that you have aided and abetted in a criminal offence, a very serious criminal offence."

"I knew what I was doing was wrong. But if you can't help someone in need, what is the point of everything. I see too much grief in this business."

"We need to know the names of your accomplices in the golf club."

"No way. If you want to charge me then do so, but I'm not involving the rest of the lads."

Billy Saunders and Ian Noble exchanged glances. "We'll leave it for the moment," said Ian Noble. "But you can expect a further visit from us."

"That's fair enough. Sorry for the extra work I'm putting on you. I realise that you lads have enough to do catching real criminals."

Billy and Ian stood up. They had got as far as the door

before Billy turned.

"Out of curiosity, what was in the coffin?"

Robbie Stephens paused. "Building materials."

"Where did the building materials come from?"

Robbie Stephens hesitated. "This will probably get me in more trouble. They were stolen from the new community centre down the Ferry, opposite the Brown's house. I suppose you'll be charging me with that as well."

"I think you're in enough trouble without worrying about a few bricks," replied Ian Noble.

Billy nodded to the receptionist as he passed through the reception area. He had not paid much attention to her before. An attractive brunette, she appeared to be in her early thirties.

The nameplate on her desk caught his eye. "Sheila Jennison, Receptionist."

CHAPTER EIGHTY TWO

Ian Noble lit up a cigarette. He and Billy were standing in the alley behind the Highland Funeral Parlour. "This is the exact spot where Davie Brown's body was found, and only one hundred yards from where Lorna was found strangled."

"Stephens is a right dodgy character, too smooth by far."

"I'll go along with that. He certainly had this town fooled for a long time. I know him as a sharp businessman and town councillor. There's been no hint of anything odd in his dealings. But this story of arranging a funeral without a body to help someone he hardly knows doesn't stack up. The whole thing smells."

"Town councillor? What exactly does Robbie Stephens do on the town council?"

"He's on the Police Liaison Committee. He's also Head of the Planning Committee."

"Is that planning, as in building development and approvals?"

"That's it."

"How long has he been Head of Planning?"

"Years."

"Ten years?"

"About that. Why?"

"It just strikes me as odd that Archie Stokes, a previous Head of Planning, was murdered. It's also too much of a coincidence that the missing Terry Thornton is, or was if he is dead, a quantity surveyor with the town council." Billy paused. "There's something I want to check out. We need to visit the Ferry."

CHAPTER EIGHTY THREE

Inverness

Billy Saunders approached the building site with caution. The previous month he had ejected the site foreman Paddy Stewart from the Merkinch Arms. Paddy was known throughout the district as a hard working foreman, but mean when he had a drink in him, which in Paddy's case happened to be most evenings. But Billy Saunders knew how to handle him. There was mutual respect between the two men. Paddy had just gone too far on the night he had been ejected. A fight had erupted between the rival fans of Celtic and Rangers over a disputed penalty award on the match being screened live on the widescreen television in the public bar. The television screen was ripped from the wall. Paddy returned the following day with a wad of money, seeking forgiveness. But that was a month ago and, as Billy knew from past experience, there was no guarantee that Paddy would be in the same peaceful temperament today.

He heard Paddy before he saw him. Paddy was hurling abuse at someone.

"Paddy, old son, how are you?" said Billy, extending his hand.

"Well. I'll be damned. If it's not Mr Scotland Yard himself. What the hell do you want here?"

"Advice, just some advice."

Five minutes later Billy Saunders left the site of the new police community centre in deep thought. He left behind him a site foreman with a puzzled look on his face.

Paddy was bewildered. Why the hell was an ex copper from the Metropolitan Police asking if any building materials had been stolen?

***

In the police car Billy and Ian discussed the next step. Paddy Stewart was adamant that no building materials were missing. His site controls were strict. Had one brick gone missing Paddy would have known.

Billy was quite clear on the next step to take. "As we have been advised by Stephens, who was the funeral director, that there is no body in the coffin, we don't require any approval for an exhumation. We simply instruct the cemetery superintendent to open the grave in a search for stolen goods."

***

Two hours later, in the presence of the cemetery superintendent, the coffin inscribed James Brown was raised to the surface.

The screws holding the coffin lid in place were undone. The stench from the open coffin was unbearable.

Billy looked at the dead body. "I think we've just found Terry Thornton."

An hour later Robbie Stephens was detained, pending further investigation into a possible murder charge. Stephens denied having anything to do with the murder of Terry Thornton.

"Which is bloody nonsense of course, as he put the body into the coffin."

"Agreed, but without Davie Brown being able to defend himself Stephens could lay the actual murder on Davie. He could say that he simply helped to dispose of the body. We need some proof that Stephens killed Thornton. Has Mrs Stephens anything to do with the funeral company?"

"Company Secretary as far as I am aware," replied Ian. "She certainly plays a big part in the business community charities."

"Detain her as well," suggested Billy, "one of them may talk."

***

When Robbie Stephens was later advised that his wife was in an adjoining cell he shrugged his shoulders in a gesture of indifference.

Four hours after Annie Stephens had been taken into custody she was released without charge. She and her husband continued to deny any involvement in the murder of Terry Thornton.

"We need a warrant, Ian. Now is the time to check the funeral parlour and the Stephens home. Without something tangible we may not have evidence to secure a murder conviction."

CHAPTER EIGHTY FOUR

Inverness

The celebrations for Tommy's release from prison, and Jimmie's return from the dead, were muted by normal Inverness standards. A coffee in Billy Saunders flat was a poor substitute for a ceilidh. Tommy and Jimmie were still trying to come to terms with the death of Davie and were in no mood for celebration.

"Two things continue to puzzle me. Who contacted Davie in Spain to inform him of the funeral? Who informed all the neighbours that Jimmie was dead? There was a helluva lot of people at that funeral. Who, apart from you two, plus Donnie Grey and Stephens, knew about the escape plan?"

"I've got to pass on that one," Jimmie replied. "As far as I'm aware the only person who knew about the funeral was Donnie Grey. It sounds daft, but I was so caught up in the plan that I never thought of asking him if anyone else was involved."

"The same goes for me Billy. All I wanted to do was get out of prison. I asked Donnie on several occasions why he had helped and I never received a satisfactory answer."

"Then there's the question of the money in the case. Where did that come from? Is it a tax evasion scam? Money laundering? Or is the money honestly earned? If so, what did Davie do to earn it? Is the money connected to the murders?"

"Well I don't know about you two, but I'm ready for a drink. In case you've both forgotten, I've just got off a murder charge. I'm sure that Davie wouldn't object."

Billy looked at Tommy.

"The case! That suitcase must have been specially made; off-the-shelf cases don't come with a secret lining. Have you any idea where Davie got the case from?"

"I've seen some people going on holiday with similar cases. They were provided free by Greggs Travel, the shop in the market. It was always part of the holiday deal that a suitcase be supplied by them. It seems odd thinking about it. Why did they insist on people taking one of their suitcases? In fact I seem to recall Davie coming home with one of the suitcases for a neighbour. I asked Davie at the time why he was delivering the case, and he said that he just happened to be in the travel shop and they asked if he would drop it in on his way home."

"What holiday deal?"

"Greggs Travel provides free holidays to some of the town folk. They send about a dozen people a year to Costa Del Sol. Some of the lucky ones get two weeks holiday."

"Have you any idea who owns Greggs Travel?"

"No idea of the owners," said Tommy, "but it's managed by Eckie and Jean MacMillan. They live in a large house in Culcabock.

Donnie pulled out his mobile phone. "I think I'll give Ian Noble a call, and make our visit to the travel shop official."

CHAPTER EIGHTY FIVE

Inverness

"For heavens sake, you can't be serious. The Macmillans are pillars of the community. They get involved in all sorts of charity work. If you keep up these suspicions there will be no business people left in the town," was the response from a flustered Ian North on being advised that the Macmillans could be tied into some sort of criminal activity.

"It could be a red herring, but I think worth following up. If you would prefer to keep out of it at the moment, then I can make discreet enquiries myself."

Ian North nodded agreement.

Billy Saunders looked at Jimmie.

"Take a trip to Greggs Travel. Work your charms with Mrs MacMillan. See if you can get a free holiday."

***

"Hi Jessie how are you? How long have you worked here?"

"Jimmie! I heard that you'd returned from the dead. What in heavens name is going on? I got a shock when Mr MacMillan told me you had died. I feel such a fool telling all the neighbours. And poor Davie being murdered. It's a wonder you're still sane."

Jimmie looked at the middle aged woman sitting at a desk covered in holiday brochures. He had known Jessie MacDonald all his life. Jessie was in her fifties, and destined to remain a spinster. Whilst God had been kind to her in the charm stakes, he had let her down badly when it came to looks.

"I'm fine. But I need your help. I need to know who

arranged Davie's holiday. He borrowed a suitcase and I want to return it."

"That would be either Mr or Mrs MacMillan. But I'm afraid they're not in the shop today. Is there anything I can do?"

"No. I just want to thank them for giving Davie a holiday. It's very charitable of them."

"But the Macmillans didn't pay for the holiday. The owner paid for it."

"Well whoever he is, he must be a real gent."

"He's certainly that, Jimmie. He's probably the only man who will ever lay hands on my body," laughed Jessie.

She looked at the puzzled expression on Jimmie's face, and laughed again. "It's Mr Stephens, the undertaker. That's what I meant about my body. I hope you didn't think…"

"Sorry Jessie, I was miles away. You mean that Robbie Stephens pays for the holidays."

"He pays for everything. He pays for the flight, provides the use of one of his villas, and gives everyone spending money. Whilst he does some business in Spain, his wife entertains the guests, which probably explains why all the guests are male. Mrs Stephens has quite a reputation with the men."

"What type of business does Robbie Stephens have in Spain?"

"Pubs, clubs, and a casino, I believe."

CHAPTER EIGHTY SIX

Billy Saunders stared out of the window of his flat. Jimmie had just finished briefing him and Tommy on the activities of Greggs Travel.

"Robbie Stephens again, and MacMillan was the conduit for advising everyone that Jimmie was supposed to be dead. What the hell are we missing?"

"Christ knows, Billy."

"Remind me of something, Tommy. How did you manage to convince the prison authorities that Jimmie was dead?"

"A solicitor turned up at the prison with a fake death certificate."

"A fake death certificate – I like the sound of that. It opens up a whole new avenue."

"The death certificate was done by Ross MacKay," stated Tommy.

"Ross MacKay? Wasn't he done for making forged bank notes back in the sixties?"

"That's the man. He was in prison with Donnie Grey. He provided Jimmie and I with the fake passports and driving licences."

"The solicitor, who was he?"

"Old man Cuthbertson, from 'Cuthbertson and Cuthbertson' in Inglis Street."

"Let's just hope that he was completely innocent in this," said Billy, "or Ian North will have my guts for garters. The way we are going there won't be enough businessmen left in Inverness for a golf foursome."

"How well do you know Ross Mackay?"

"I went to primary school with him, but have had no dealings with him since then. He's lived in the same run down house in the Hill district for over fifty years. Bit of a recluse.

He tends to wander around in a torn anorak, dirty jeans and old trainers."

"Well I think it's time you renewed your acquaintance with him."

CHAPTER EIGHTY SEVEN

Inverness

Billy Saunders pushed open the gate leading onto the driveway of the large house. One glance had been enough to tell him that the house was badly in need of a major refurbishment. The garden would have tested the efforts of a Ground Force squadron.

The plan had been discussed beforehand. Tommy would go to the front door, whilst Billy and Jimmie searched the rear of the house and the outbuildings.

It took Tommy five minutes to get an answer to his persistent knocking. Ross MacKay answered the door. He was wearing a dressing gown and slippers. Tommy looked at his watch. It was five o'clock in the afternoon.

It took Ross MacKay three minutes to convince Tommy that he wasn't interested in renewing old primary school acquaintances. The discussion reached a finale when Ross MacKay slammed the door in Tommy's face, with the comment – "What part of sod off don't you understand?"

***

The discovery was made by Billy in the basement of the large house. A printing press, treasury bank paper, inks, and plates for various denominations of Euro notes, were located in one corner of the large well lit basement. A number of empty packing crates were stacked by the work bench, as though in anticipation of an imminent departure. Whatever domestic skills Ross MacKay may have been lacking were not evident in his work environment. The printing set up was in pristine condition. Ross MacKay clearly took pride in his work.

"I can't see MacKay letting us into the house Billy. He wasn't too happy when I knocked on his door."

"Well, we have to get into the house somehow, before he scarpers."

"It's up to you Jimmie."

"Okay, you two wait here."

***

Two minutes later Jimmie returned.

"That's it, the back door is open."

Ross MacKay put up no resistance when confronted.

Ian Noble arrived on the scene ten minutes later.

Ross MacKay confessed to being part of a money laundering operation. The forged Euro notes were taken out to Spain on the free holidays organised by Stephens and Greggs Travel without the knowledge of the holidaymakers. Whilst Annie Stephens attended to the whims of her guests in Spain, her husband laundered the money through his legitimate Spanish businesses. Genuine banknotes came back to Britain in the suitcase lining.

Involved in the conspiracy were Ross MacKay, Robbie and Annie Stephens, Davie Brown and the Macmillans.

When Ross MacKay was advised that in addition to money laundering charges he would also be charged with being involved in the murder of Terry Thornton he broke down. A full confession followed.

His statement incriminated Robbie Stephens in the murder of Terry Thornton. He also stated that Stephens had boasted how he had got rid of Davie Brown, and that both Annie and Robbie Stephens were involved in the killing of Archie Stokes and Lorna Reid.

Two days later two senior officers from Scotland Yard arrived in Inverness to interview the Stephens about a series of murders committed in the London area in the seventies and eighties.

***

Billy Saunders was in attendance when the police search of the funeral parlour was undertaken. In a drawer containing a number of watches, rings, and other items of jewellery, he came across Lorna Reid's bracelet. He had given it to Lorna the day before she was murdered. It had been his mother's bracelet. It was the only thing he had kept, when he had cleared out his father's home, following the death of his father.

"It looks as though Stephens was stripping the dead before he buried them," was Ian Noble's comment.

CHAPTER EIGHTY EIGHT

Inverness

Three days after formal charges had been made and statements had been taken from Ross MacKay and the Macmillans, Billy Saunders and Ian Noble reflected on the events surrounding the deaths of Terry Thornton, Davie Brown, Archie Stokes and Lorna Reid.

"Despite the refusal of the Stephens to make a statement we have a good idea of the sequence of events. We know that ten years ago Robbie Stephens was next in line for the Head of Planning position. But in order for Stephens to get the position, Archie Stokes had to step down. Robbie and Annie Stephens visited Stokes at his home, possibly with a view to getting him to resign voluntarily. When Stokes refused to resign he was murdered. Robbie Stephens then took over the senior position on the planning committee. He was totally bent, and found it easy to say "yes" when approached by corrupt contractors. For the past ten years he has systematically used his authority to sway planning decisions in favour of his preferred contractors."

"Where does Eddie Jackson figure in all of this?"

"A couple of days after killing Stokes, the Stephens were asked to make the funeral arrangements for Eddie Jackson, who had died of natural causes. Stephens knew that Jackson was a career burglar, and saw an opportunity. He knew it was safe to return to Stokes' house after the murder and before the body was found, as Stokes lived on his own. At this stage, nobody was too perturbed at Stokes missing one council meeting. Stephens placed Jackson's prints on a piece of marble whilst Jackson was being prepared for his funeral. He removed Jackson's signet ring from his dead body, and took the ring and the piece of marble to Stokes' house. Wearing gloves he forced the marble into Stokes' head wound before leaving the marble and the ring by the window. He then broke the window to give the impression of a burglary, after which he removed the video recorder and picture from Stokes' house. He later placed these items in Jackson's house, when he visited the house, to make the final funeral arrangements. A few days later, when Stokes failed to turn up for another council meeting, Stephens suggested that someone visit Stokes' house to make sure he was okay. By this time the stage was set for Stephens to take on the role of Head of Planning, with Jackson carrying the can for the murder of Archie Stokes."

"I'm with you so far. But why was Lorna killed?"

"Lorna realised what the murder weapon was. It was a piece of marble, but of a different shape to the one found by the body. It wasn't a paperweight. It was actually a marble sample for a headstone. I saw similar samples in Stephen's reception area, when we visited his office. It was obvious what it really was, just not the kind of thing you see on a day to day basis. Stephens must have had some samples in his briefcase when he visited Stokes. That would explain the blood stains we found in his briefcase. He must have disposed of the real murder weapon as soon as he left Stokes' house after the murder. Lorna realised what the murder weapon was on the night she was killed. When she tried to contact me before her lecture she was excited at her discovery. She must have said something to Annie Stephens at the Ladies' Institute lecture which alarmed her. Annie Stephens threw us off the scent with the nonsense about Stokes accosting women. I suspect that she lured Lorna back to the funeral parlour on the pretext of looking at the marble samples. Robbie Stephens was there and he strangled Lorna. I should have realised the connection before. I detected a familiar smell in Lorna's car the night she was killed. The smell was formaldehyde. Stephens must have been preparing a body for burial when Lorna turned up. He killed her, dumped her in her car which was parked just outside the funeral parlour, and drove it around the corner to Queensgate."

"So where does Terry Thornton come into the picture?"

"As a quantity surveyor working for the council Terry Thornton became concerned about several of the contracts that Stephens had awarded, and approached him at the funeral parlour one evening. We know from Ross MacKay's statement that Davie Brown was at the funeral parlour on the same evening. We know that Davie became involved in the money laundering, when he burgled the MacMillan home several years ago and found a great deal of money. The money laundering consortium could see a use for Davie, even if it was just identifying candidates for the holiday. Davie was paid peanuts compared to the rest, but it bought his silence. He turned up at the funeral parlour just in time to witness the murder of Terry Thornton. Davie panicked at the sight of the dead body. To get Davie out of the way, Robbie Stephens sent Davie to Spain the following day. The body of Terry Thornton was placed in the mortuary, whilst Stephens decided what to do with it. Stephens probably couldn't believe his luck when Tommy Brown was arrested for the murder of Terry Thornton. He later heard, from the police clerk, that Tommy was to be released due to lack of evidence, and came up with the idea of effecting Tommy's escape by staging Jimmie's funeral. Staging Jimmie's funeral enabled him to dispose of Thornton's body. Getting Tommy on the run, and planting additional evidence, implicated Tommy even further."

"But why did Stephens murder Davie Brown?"

"Davie knew too much. Stephens wanted him back from Costa Del Sol to silence him. He got the Macmillans to phone Davie in Spain to say that Jimmie was dead. The Macmillans used Jessie Macdonald to tell all the neighbours about the funeral. Not ones to miss an opportunity Stephens and Davie put counterfeit Euro notes in Davie's suitcase for the trip to Spain, and Davie returned with the genuine banknotes. Davie's admission to hospital delayed his murder. When

Davie was in hospital Ross MacKay visited Davie's home to retrieve the case containing the money. But by this time the suitcase was on the way to Chatham. When he discharged himself from hospital and visited the funeral parlour he must have threatened to expose Stephens. Stephens chased him into the alley and murdered him. Stephens was interrupted during the killing and had to leave the body in the alley."

"What was Donnie Grey's involvement?"

"We know that Andy Spiers had initially moved to London from Chatham. In London, Stanton worked as a prostitute with Spiers presumably acting as her pimp. I have no doubt that Spiers assisted Stanton in the murders committed in London. When Stanton's name was put in the frame for the murders they decided to move again. I suspect that Spiers ran into Donnie Grey in London, after Donnie came out of prison. Donnie probably talked about his time in Inverness, and mentioned Ross MacKay's name. Andy Spiers had enough money, and the knowledge, to open up a funeral parlour. Within days of arriving in Inverness, Spiers contacted Ross MacKay and bought new identities from him. Andy Spiers and Ann Stanton became Mr and Mrs Robbie Stephens. They then opened the funeral parlour and blended into the business community. Donnie Grey had left Inverness the previous year. This suited the Stephens, as it meant that nobody in Inverness knew who they really were."

"Stephens got his receptionist Sheila Jennison to contact Shona Grey's old neighbour in Inverness to get Shona's telephone number in Kent. Sheila Jennison innocently phoned Donnie Grey with the intention of handing the call to Robbie Stephens when Donnie answered the phone. It must have been quite a shock for Donnie Grey to hear the name Sheila Jennison after all these years. Stephens demanded Donnie's help in staging Jimmie Brown's funeral, and planting evidence. He gave no reason why he wanted this done. He made no mention of Terry Thornton's murder or the money laundering. But Donnie had built a new life for himself. When Donnie initially refused to help, Stephens threatened to inform Donnie's wife that he had been engaged in criminal activity in his youth. We know about the drug dealing, but there was possibly something much more serious that Stephens threatened to expose. Perhaps Donnie had told him something in a drunken moment. Whatever it was, Donnie was concerned about Shona finding out. Stephens then put the frighteners on Donnie by saying his family would be hurt. Donnie Grey gave in. He came to Inverness, and assisted in the staged funeral."

"Stephens placed Terry Thornton's blood and fingerprints on a knife whilst Thornton's body was in the funeral parlour, in the same way as he had Jackson's. When Tommy got into the hearse, on his escape from the cemetery, he found the knife lying on his seat. He moved the knife, leaving his prints. Donnie Grey, wearing gloves, picked up the knife, and left it at Tommy's house, where it was found by the police."

"Sheila Jennison, the receptionist, where does she fit into all of this?"

"I visited her at her home. She is completely innocent. She had only been working at the funeral parlour for a month. She has no idea that Donnie Grey went out with her mother in the seventies and that Donnie was her father. Her mother lives with her in a cottage at Ardersier. They both came across as very nice people. Her mother still goes for treatment at the mental hospital but I saw no signs of any vindictiveness. She still carries a torch for Donnie Grey however. There was a photograph in the living room of her and Donnie taken in the sixties."

"What about Donnie Grey? Did he commit suicide?"

"I'm not sure. Everything appeared to get on top of him. He may have felt that the only way to protect his family was to top himself. I'm not completely convinced however. We now know that MacInver died in prison eight years ago, so that eliminates him as a possible killer of Donnie."

"Are you holding something back Billy?"

"A couple of things are bothering me. Once I find the

answers to these, I will be a lot easier in my mind. I'll give Ted Williams a ring in Chatham, and let him know how it was all resolved at this end."

CHAPTER EIGHTY NINE

Inverness

Billy, Tommy and Jimmie were holding a muted celebration in the MacEwans Arms. Davie was still uppermost in their minds. A very pregnant Elsie Rooney was also in the bar with Alastair Winngate. Alastair's charms were clearly a more effective aphrodisiac to Elsie than Jimmie's miraculous return from the dead.

"It's probably not my sprog anyway," declared an indifferent Jimmie.

"She's probably still in denial over your death," remarked Billy.

"Denial, the daft cow doesn't know the meaning of the word. She probably thinks it's a river in Egypt."

"Well, Tommy, what are you going to do about Hamish MacGregor? The police are expecting him at the station with his driving licence and insurance documents any day now."

"They called at the house yesterday afternoon looking for him. I said he was in Aberdeen. I don't know how I am going to get out of this one."

"How about this, Dad?" said Jimmie, holding up a piece of paper.

"What's that?"

"A death certificate, it just needs filling in."

"Where did you get that from?"

"I paid a visit to Ross MacKay's house last night."

"Great. I can tell the police that Hamish died in Aberdeen. I'll send a copy of the death certificate to North Sea Oil and terminate the pension. I've been riding my luck far too long with this pension scam. The down side of course is that my pension will stop. What the hell am I going to live on now?"

"Try this for starters."

Tommy looked at the bundle of banknotes that Jimmie had thrown in his lap.

"Where did this come from?"

"Ross MacKay didn't believe in banks, nor did he spend any money. He hid his share of the money laundering proceeds in his home. He made quite a few bob out of the racket."

CHAPTER NINETY

Chatham, December 2000

She looked at the inscription on the headstone.

Elaine Jessica Ash
Died 4 May 1947
Age 3 Years
Safe in the arms of Jesus

After nearly sixty years she could still hear her mother saying that had it not been for the drunken doctor, Elaine would have lived. The doctor had been so drunk when he arrived at the house that he made a wrong diagnosis. "Just a head cold," he had said. Two hours later Elaine was dead.

It had taken her more than thirty years to exact her revenge. Killing the doctor in 1980 had been easy. She had waited long enough.

"Let's go love. If you wish we can come back next week with some flowers," the man said.

Chrissie turned and looked at the man. They had been married nearly eighteen years. He had been there when she needed him. It was difficult to believe just how much she hated him.

CHAPTER NINETY ONE

Inverness, February 2001

Billy Saunders glanced through the newspaper as he waited for a response from the records clerk at Scotland Yard. It had taken three months of patient waiting before he had asked the question. The timing had to be right. But a call to Chatham police the previous day had confirmed that the main stumbling block had been removed. This had encouraged him to proceed, in the knowledge that there was a chance that his request would be listened to.

He cast the newspaper to one side and looked at his watch. He had been on the telephone for fifteen minutes. The same clerk had answered the telephone two hours earlier, and had been unhelpful, pointing out that they had enough paperwork on current crimes being handled by serving policemen, without the need to look into crimes committed in the sixties, at the request of a retired officer.

In the end Billy had to use his contacts in the Yard. A call to an old friend in the Central Drugs Squad had resulted in the clerk being visited by an undercover officer. Being confronted by a large skinhead, requesting the information, had encouraged the clerk to phone Billy, asking that Billy repeat his earlier request. The records clerk must have moved heaven and earth to get the information Billy wanted. Billy wondered exactly what the Drugs Squad officer had said to the clerk to justify such service.

"Are you still there?"

"I'm here. Any luck?"

"Yes. I think I have all the information that you need. The paper is a bit faded but the writing is discernible. I'm not sure if it will be legible if I transmit it by fax. I could post a copy of it to you this afternoon."

"Try the fax. I don't need the document as evidence. I just want to refresh my memory."

"OK. It'll be with you in ten minutes. Give me your fax number."

***

Billy glanced at the list. The names from the sixties flooded back. He had been right. He read through the second document. It was also as he remembered.

He picked up the telephone.

Roy Rogers answered on the first ring.

CHAPTER NINETY TWO

Chatham, February 2001

A week after Billy Saunders telephoned Roy Rogers, the two were shaking hands in the reception area of the Bridgewood Manor Hotel. Jimmie Brown accompanied Billy on his trip south. Jimmie wanted to renew acquaintances with Petty Cash.

"I'm sorry to impose on you Roy, but I believe there are still quite a lot of questions that need answering. I'm not convinced that going through formal channels at this stage will help matters."

"Well I must admit I'm intrigued, although I can see why you had to wait for Ted Williams to retire before asking the questions."

"It would have been impossible to make enquiries with Williams still on the scene. Where has he retired to?"

"The Algarve I believe."

"Here are the names that I want you to check. I need to know if these people were arrested in the sixties for drug dealing, and if they have any record since then. What I find odd is that, when I mentioned Andy Spiers' name to Ted Williams, he did not react on hearing the name. He also failed to mention the connection between Spiers and Ann Stanton."

Roy Rogers pulled a battered spectacle case from his pocket. "Age. My eyes are the last bit to go. The rest of me has been knackered for years. I think I'll get out of the force in the next few months and get some time with the grandchildren."

Roy looked at the list of names. He looked up after a few seconds. "You already know about Grey, of course, about his apparent suicide at the end of last year. Andy Spiers has no record with the Kent Police although, in my opinion, he should have been locked up several times. The other three are interesting."

"Interesting, in what way?"

"This Reginald Allder. I don't think he had ever been arrested, but if it's the bloke I'm thinking of, he was murdered in the sixties."

"Murdered?"

"Yes, and it gets better. John Piper, another name on the list. His body was uncovered only four months ago. He has been dead for thirty or forty years."

"So, out of a list of five, we have one in prison charged with multiple murders, one apparent suicide, and two murdered. Yet none of them had any convictions?"

"I can't speak for Piper. He was a naval officer. But I haven't finished yet. The fifth man, Roy Gibson, died a few months ago. The brakes on his car failed."

"Roy Gibson lived in Medway?"

"Yes, in Chatham."

"This is too much of a coincidence."

"Fancy a drink? I think I need one."

Billy placed the empty glass on the table.

"It's a long shot, but was Ted Williams ever involved in any unsolved crimes? I accept that there will always be unsolved crimes, but have there been any serious crimes in the Medway area, where Williams was involved, and where he could have been paid to turn a blind eye?"

"That's a bit extreme isn't it? Ted Williams came across as a good officer."

"These names I gave you were all drug dealers, allegedly arrested by Williams in the sixties. I would like to know why he made a statement, saying that they had all been arrested, when they weren't. That is not the action of an honest copper."

"I'll dig around when I go into the station tomorrow. The records are now computerised but I had the task of collating the information for the computer. I even got stuffed with the job of organising the paper record archives. However…"

"What is it?"

"A colleague of mine, Bob Smithers, made an odd comment about the Grey suicide. Ted Williams' name was mentioned. I'll give Bob a ring when I get home and ask him to come and see you here. But we'd better keep quiet about what we're doing. I've got my pension to think about."

CHAPTER NINETY THREE

Chatham

"So you're Inspector Saunders of the Yard, I've heard a great deal about you."

"Ex Inspector. A humble civilian now, but still sticking my nose in. It's good to meet you Bob."

"Roy said that you wanted to see this report into the death of Donnie Grey."

"I'll order some coffee whilst I glance through it."

***

"Well, that all seems straightforward. According to your report Grey was seen to jump from the fourth floor of a building by a schoolboy. I'd heard that already. So what's the problem?"

"The report is factual. What it does not tell you is the feel for the situation."

"What do you mean?"

"I arrived on the scene within a couple of minutes of the body being found. I was only there a matter of seconds when my senior officer turned up."

"Who would that be?"

"Chief Inspector Ted Williams. I was taken aback, because as far as I was aware, he was supposed to be working at regional headquarters in Maidstone."

"Did he do anything at the scene?"

"He checked the fourth floor from where Grey jumped. I then did the same thing and completed my report. It just struck me as odd."

"What?"

"He just seemed to materialise out of nowhere. I never thought of asking him what he was doing there, and made no mention of it in my report. He reached the same conclusion as I did, that it was probably suicide."

"Who reached the conclusion first?"

"Difficult to say, he could have suggested it, I suppose. The statement from the schoolboy is quite clear. Grey jumped from the fourth floor."

"This schoolboy, is his school local?"

"Just down the road. Why?"

"Could you come with me, I'd like to run through his statement with him. I'll need an official police presence."

***

An hour later, in front of the school headmaster, ten year old James York admitted that he had lied, when he said that he had seen Donnie Grey jump from a window.

CHAPTER NINETY FOUR

Chatham, February 2001

It took Roy Rogers two days to come back to Billy, but when he did he had an armful of files.

"There's another lot in the car."

"Hold on, Jimmie and I'll give you a hand."

"That's it, a total of sixteen cases spanning thirty six years. The total number of unsolved cases of serious crimes in that time is closer to a hundred. I skimmed through these and came down to those sixteen as worth looking at, because Ted Williams was involved in each investigation."

"Let's break them down, murders on one pile, robberies in another, and the other crimes lumped together. Let's start with the murders."

"I realised the files would take some time to read through, so I prepared a brief resume of just the murder cases."

Roy handed a sheet of paper to Billy and Jimmie.

"I've put them in chronological order."

1. James Lewis, a 38 year old supermarket check out operator, murdered in November 1964 on Luton Recreation Ground, Chatham. He suffered extensive injuries to his head. A married man with two sons aged fourteen and ten. He had been in the Luton Tavern pub for an hour and a half earlier in the evening. He was on his way home when he was murdered.
2. Andrew Lawson, a 39 year old civil servant from Gillingham. Worked with Gillingham Council. His body was found in playing fields behind the municipal centre in April 1967. Beaten to death with

a proverbial blunt instrument. He was in the Prince Albert pub earlier in the evening. A married man with one son aged eleven.

3. Bert Woodlands, an unemployed electrician. Age 42. Lived in Rainham. Found in an alley off Rainham High Street in October 1975. He was stabbed to death. Earlier in the evening he had an argument with a local builder in the Railway Tavern. The builder was questioned but he had a sound alibi. Woodlands was known as a heavy drinker. Married with two children, a boy of eleven, and a girl of sixteen."
4. Sydney Cooper, a 36 year old Rainham bank clerk. His body was found in the gents toilet at a local shopping centre in May 1979. Stabbed to death. He had been out shopping. His shopping bag was with the body. Married with two children, a girl aged twelve and a boy aged ten.
5. Doctor Eric Anderton, age 62 from Hempstead. Found strangled with a necktie in June 1986 in a playing field close to a public house, where he had spent most of his last evening. A widower, he lived fifty yards from where he was murdered."
6. Doctor Andrew Harris. Age 59. Found strangled with a necktie in Chatham Library car park in February1995. He had been in the Conservative Club attending a social function. A married man."

"So the first murder was in 1964 and the last in 1995. That makes six killings in thirty one years. No regular pattern in the way the victims died. Is there a link between them, or are they just isolated killings brought together simply because Ted Williams happened to be one of the investigating officers?"

"He was the senior investigating officer in the last three killings. The force was under such a workload that even junior officers had to assume senior investigating roles."

"Right, let's see if there is any pattern with them."

"Geography, how far apart are the murders?"

"No more than five miles."

"Age range between thirty six and sixty two. Too wide a range to have any significance."

"Apart from one, they were all in steady employment."

"According to the files, none of them knew any of the others."

"So in summary, six men from six different walks of life, apart from the two doctors, all total strangers to each other, with nothing in common."

Jimmie Brown lay sprawled in an easy chair. He had been listening to the exchange between Billy and Roy. "Can I put in a couple of bobs worth?"

"What is it Jimmie?"

"What was in the shopping bag found in the toilet?"

"What's the relevance of that?"

"Just humour me, Roy. Is there a note in the file?"

Roy flicked through the file for Sydney Cooper. "Bread, coffee, cat food, and a bottle of whisky."

"Alcohol, that's a possible connection. All of those murdered had either just been in a pub, club or off-licence. Have these blokes got form? Have they ever been in trouble with the police? Have they ever upset Ted Williams at some stage?"

"Hold on Jimmie. I'm supposed to be the detective here."

"It's the work I do with computers. I've trained myself to look for links between things."

Roy picked up one of the files. "Let's check through the files to see if any of them have form. If we take two files each it'll only take a few minutes."

***

It was thirty minutes before conversation was resumed.

"Six murders, and in four instances the victim had been cautioned for being drunk and disorderly a week prior to his death."

"And in each case the cautioning officer was Ted Williams."

"And in each case the victim was one of the younger men."

"Now that is just too much of a coincidence."

"There is one other thing."

"What's that Jimmie?"

"All the victims who received a caution had a son aged ten or eleven. It could be nothing, but it may have some significance."

"How can we find out about Ted Williams' background, Roy?"

"I'll have a word with my mother. She's lived in Chatham all her life and is a bigger know-all than I am."

"Thanks, Roy."

"Perhaps we are looking for a tee-total avenger?"

Billy looked up sharply at Jimmie's comment. He recalled Ted Williams' views on alcohol.

Roy Rogers stood up. "I'm going back to the station. I need to check on an old Missing Person report."

"Okay, Roy. Thanks for all your help."

***

Later that day Roy contacted Billy.

"Ted Williams' father was known locally as a drunkard and a bully. He had been picked-up and cautioned on several occasions but was released without charge on each occasion. He had a bad name in the town. He died nearly fifty years ago when Ted Williams was about ten years of age."

"I wonder if that was sufficient motivation for Ted Williams to extract revenge on drunken fathers? Perhaps he was abused by his father and didn't want other kids to suffer."

"Heaven knows, it's strange what goes on in people's minds."

"That still leaves the question of the two doctors. Are

these deaths connected? Are they connected to Ted Williams?"

"I see that one of the doctors was a member of the Conservative Club. Did Ted Williams have any political views?" commented Jimmie.

"He was well known for his strong political views. He hated this present government. He always maintained that Margaret Thatcher was still the one to sort the country out."

"So he could have been a member of the Conservative club?"

"He was not only a member. He was the local chairman," interjected Roy. "I have one further bit of news, Billy. I checked the Missing Person report for young Jack Watson, the chap whose body was found with Petty Officer Piper's body. The person who reported him missing was his girl-friend Chrissie Ash."

"And the significance of that?"

"Chrissie Ash is married to Ted Williams."

"Chrissie! Christine! Well that has to be of some significance. I think it's time I paid a visit to Scotland Yard."

"I won't offer to come with you Billy. I'm allergic to police stations."

"With your track record Jimmie, I'm not surprised."

CHAPTER NINETY FIVE

London, March 2001

"Let me get this straight. You are saying that one of the longest serving officers in the Kent Constabulary, an officer who has received the MBE, has for nearly forty years been systematically carrying out serious criminal offences, and you are basing these allegations on flimsy circumstantial evidence."

"Hardly flimsy," replied Billy Saunders, looking across the desk at Chief Superintendent John Worthing.

Worthing stood up and grimaced. As senior officer in charge of internal police investigations in the Metropolitan Police he had come across many instances of bent coppers. But what Billy Saunders had related to him in the previous ten minutes stretched the boundaries of incredulity.

"This business in the sixties, the raid on the drugs factory in London. That was a long time ago. How can you possibly expect Ted Williams to have remembered the names after all this time?"

"The drugs raid was very high profile for both our careers. Hardly the type of thing we would forget. I repeatedly mentioned Spiers' and Grey's names to Ted Williams but got no reaction from him. When I informed him last September that Andrew Roger Spiers had been charged with several murders he reacted as though he had never heard the name before. Not once did he mention Spiers' name in connection with Ann Stanton, even in the eighties."

"You do realise that this is outside my jurisdiction. I will need something solid, before I go to the Chief Constable of Kent."

"If that was my only reason I would not have troubled you, I would have put my doubts down to old age. But, taken with the other issues I raised, I believe there is justification for contacting Maidstone."

"Ah yes! The other issues. This business of one of the dealers you mentioned committing suicide last year."

"According to the official report into the death of Donald Grey, the first officer on the scene was Sergeant Smithers. I recently had a face to face meeting with Smithers, and ran through his report with him. It turns out that he omitted to mention that Ted Williams was also at the scene. In fact Ted Williams was the first officer to walk the scene. A ten year old schoolboy who professed to be a witness to the whole thing admitted later that he had fabricated the story of seeing Grey jump from the fourth floor. A scene of crime team has since carried out a check of the building. It had been sealed immediately after the fall, to prevent a repeat occurrence. The scene was therefore as it had been on the day of the incident. The forensic team established that there had been no disturbance in that area, although there were footprints. Despite this, it is my belief that Ted Williams murdered Grey, and then pushed him out of the window to make it look like suicide."

"Why would Williams murder Grey? Is this where the naval petty officer and the other chap come into the picture?"

"That's it. In the early sixties Chatham police received reports of two missing people. One of them was the naval petty officer on the drugs list. It was assumed at the time that he had deserted. The second missing person was a young man named Jack Watson, who is an innocent victim of circumstances. When the bodies were found last year, Ted Williams put himself in charge of the investigation. Williams paperwork is missing. A report on the finding of the bodies was independently prepared by the police pathologist. He confirmed that the bodies were those of Piper and Watson. The bodies were identified from dental records."

"But what makes you believe that Williams was involved with these deaths?"

"Just a gut feeling. He is married to Jack Watson's old

girl-friend."

"That could be just a coincidence. What about the murders in Medway and London?"

"A gut feeling again. It all points to Ted Williams. He was abused as a child by his father. This could have given him the urge for revenge, killings drunken fathers. I don't know where the murder of the doctors comes into it. We now know that Ann Stanton was in Inverness during these murders. My guess is that Williams used the modus operandi for the London killing, a necktie, to cast the blame onto Stanton. I have no idea why he picked on doctors. But this is just pure speculation."

"I'm not completely convinced. You've made a great deal of assumptions based on very little evidence. It could be just a coincidence that the murder victims in Kent had all been cautioned by Ted Williams. You've made a great leap from him being physically abused by his father to killing people. Bring me something more concrete and I'll follow it through."

Billy stood up.

"I'm not sure what else I can produce."

"Well I'll leave it with you. Let me know if anything develops."

CHAPTER NINETY SIX

The Algarve, April 2001

Ted Williams looked at the manuscript. It had taken him three months to produce the fifty thousand words. He had never contemplated writing a book, let alone an autobiography. But when he had been told about the cancer, he decided that he had to leave his story. He regretted not having retired earlier. It would have given him more time with Christine. Eight weeks would not be enough. The grim reaper was already sharpening his scythe.

He looked once again at the manuscript. It was a pity he would never see the published article. He was certain that it would find a publisher. It made good reading. The public loved to read about bent coppers. He would stick to the police angle however. He did not want the whole world to know that he was abused as a child. He was ten years of age before God had answered his prayer. He had gone to the funfair at the Strand when he was told that his father had died as the result of car accident. It was the happiest day of his life.

Over the next few days he would make enquiries about a publisher. In the meantime he would get rid of the hard copy. There was no point in leaving anything incriminating lying around. He would send a software copy to his solicitor in London in a couple of weeks, with the instruction to forward it to a publisher after his death. He would make sure that Christine was not mentioned in his confession.

He pulled the shredder closer to the coffee table and picked up the large malt whisky.

***

He had been secretly in love with Christine Ash since

primary school days. How he had hated that name Chrissie. Her name was Christine. She had never even noticed him, despite the fact that he was the tallest boy in the school. He had even held her hand at the funeral of Ian Thorn, the classmate who had drowned on a school outing. Her mind had always seemed to be on something other than school. It was probably something to do with Elaine's death. Christine was only six, and in her second year of primary school, when her little sister had died. It was the talk of the school for weeks.

Christine had gone to a different secondary school from him, and he had lost touch with her for ten years. Until the day he had arrested Donnie Grey at the NAAFI Club for beating up the barman at the Fountain Inn, because the barman had upset Donnie's sister by ditching her. It was wonderful seeing Christine after all those years, even though she was with another man. He had not expected Donnie Grey to be so co-operative. Within minutes of being in the interview room, Grey had confessed to a number of crimes. He could see a future use for Grey.

***

Billy Saunders was an inspiration in the early sixties, when the Met Police had bust the drugs factory in Plaistow. When Saunders had briefed him on how much money could be made manufacturing and selling drugs, he decided that he wanted a piece of the action. When Saunders had gone on compassionate leave, and was temporarily out of the picture, he had discreetly visited the Plaistow drugs factory and had met the main man, Roy Gibson. He alerted Gibson to the planned raid. Most of the stock had then been moved out of the factory. The manufacturing team were not alerted to the raid, on the basis that if they were arrested, the police would assume that the whole operation had been closed down. He had arrested the dealers in Maidstone, Ashford and Margate. He had retained the dealers in Chatham, but working directly for him and Gibson. Only Reginald Allder had refused to go along with it. He was quickly silenced. Donnie Grey and Piper were already on his payroll. A month later he and Gibson had opened up a new factory in Chatham, where he could keep an eye on any police interest in the activities. Petty Officer Piper had been only one of several useful navy contacts. At the peak of the business he had forty dealers covering the south of England, with a manufacturing unit in Chatham and Gravesend. Only Roy Gibson had known that he was the key man in the operation. He had read the newspaper report about Gibson's car accident. Faulty brakes they had said. That had tied up all the loose ends. The flowers on Gibson's grave were still fresh on the day he visited the cemetery with Christine.

He made sure that no charges were brought against Donnie Grey for the assault on the barman in the Fountain Inn. He had also made sure that Andy Spiers was never made aware of his activities. There was something dangerous about Spiers. It came as no surprise when Billy Saunders contacted him, to tell him that Spiers had committed several murders.

***

Donnie Grey killing Jack Watson was fortuitous. It meant that Christine was no longer courting. But Jack deserting her, as she believed he had done, had affected her mind. Killing Petty Officer Piper was necessary. He became hysterical when he saw Jack Watson being killed. Like Watson, Piper never felt the knife enter his heart. The grave was almost ready. He and Donnie Grey had only had to dig a further two feet into the drainage trench and cover the bodies with soil. It was funny, in a morbid sort of way, seeing John Piper's white hand stick out of the soil. A couple of thumps from the spade had soon sorted out that little problem. Being involved in the killing of Watson and Piper resulted in Donnie Grey leaving the Medway area. The Admiralty police were on to Piper anyway. It would only have been a matter of time before they acted.

***

He was the officer on duty when the call came in from Doctor Bills' neighbour, saying that there were strange noises coming from the doctor's house. He had gone to investigate, and had found Christine sitting at the foot of the stairs, with the dead doctor beside her. He nearly wept as he comforted her. It took him two hours to clean up the mess and take Christine home. He then returned to the doctor's house and re-arranged the body. His report stated that the doctor appeared to have fallen down the stairs whilst drunk, and had struck his head several times on the wooden banisters. In the absence of any evidence to the contrary, the coroner had agreed that the finding would be "Accidental Death." He sympathised with Christine, when she explained why she had killed the doctor. He would have done the same thing. When she had seen him several years before, in the police car outside the NAAFI Club, handcuffed to another man, she had assumed that he was a prisoner.

He and Christine had married the following year. He had no regrets about killing the drunken fathers. They would only have turned out like his father. He had to protect the children. But Christine had changed him. He had left the fathers alone after that. Instead he helped Christine in her mission with the doctors. He quite enjoyed helping her.

***

It was quite a shock seeing Donnie Grey in the public house after all those years. He could see that Grey recognised him. When Grey contacted him the next day, he met him in the public house and assured him that there was nothing to worry about. It was all in the past. Best forget it. But when Grey telephoned him twenty years later after the discovery of Piper and Watson's remains, saying that Billy Saunders was asking questions, he could see that Grey was close to breaking point and had to be silenced. He met Grey at the

Historic Dockyard. It had been a close thing. The nosey school kid who found Grey's body had nearly seen him as he pushed, the already dead, Grey out of the window. Thank heavens Sergeant Smithers had turned up at the crime scene before a more competent officer. It had been a close thing when the kid stated that he had seen the man jump out of the fourth floor window. The murder had actually taken place on the third floor. But the kid's fantasy gave him the chance to go up to the fourth floor and leave one set of scuffed footprints leading to the window. A quick tidy up on the third floor on the way back down to Sergeant Smithers and the crime scene was obliterated. A gentle hint to the sergeant on the need to check the fourth floor had resulted in the sergeant submitting a report that the death appeared to be suicide. He made sure that Christine did not read about the unearthing of Jack Williams body by sending her on holiday for two weeks. What she didn't know wouldn't hurt her.

***

It was a pity that he and Christine had never had children. The complications during her miscarriage when she was carrying Jack Watson's baby meant that she could never have any children.

"Just as well," he muttered to himself, "what child would want a couple of psychopaths as parents."

He finished shredding the manuscript and went into the study.

He sat down at the laptop and opened up the bank details. With nearly three million pounds in a Swiss bank account he could afford to do what he wanted. It was a pity he did not have any time left to enjoy the fruits of his illegal activities.

He smiled as Christine approached with a bottle of his favourite malt. He really did love her. He wished he did not give her such a hard time.

CHAPTER NINETY SEVEN

Inverness, April 2001

Three days after his visit to Scotland Yard, Billy Saunders was in the Merkinch Arms with Tommy and Jimmie Brown.

"Ever play golf Jimmie?"

"Not really my scene. I was in the Inverness Golf Club once, but I managed to get out before the police arrived."

"Do you have any of the money that you nicked from Ross Mackay's house?"

"How much do you need?"

"I don't need it, but I think you and I should go to the Algarve. Do you have a passport?"

"Yes. It's in the name of David Young."

***

A week later Billy and Jimmie arrived at the Palmares Golf Club. The golf club and the four star Hotel Galfino were to Jimmie's taste.

"Tomorrow morning we'll visit Ted Williams. He'll get a surprise."

CHAPTER NINETY EIGHT

The Algarve, April 2001

Christine Williams stared into the water. Five minutes had passed since the last bubble had risen to the surface. Her arm was aching. Holding down a fifteen stone body was hard work.

She looked into the water and slowly released her hand, expecting Ted to jump out.

But he was dead. There was no doubt about it.

It had been much easier holding Ian Thorn under the water when they were in primary school. Thorn had gone too far when he had said something about Elaine. Nobody was looking. The swimming pool was busy and noisy. It had only taken a minute.

***

Ted Williams had been a bully all their married life. Even worse, he thought that she was stupid.

When she returned from her two week holiday the previous September the first thing she did was pick up her periodicals at the newsagent. The newsagent saved her a copy of Woman's Weekly and The Chatham Standard every week.

She had read the article about the discovery of the two skeletons. As soon as she read about the Timex watch, she knew it was Jack. She recalled seeing Ted as he strode down the path towards the Command House with two other men, one of them in naval uniform, on the same day that Jack had disappeared.

***

She had been surprised to see Ted at Doctor Bill's house. But she remembered who he was – the big creepy chap who used to stare at her in school. When he started clearing up the murder scene she went along with it. She had to marry him in the end. He just wouldn't take no for an answer.

Still, he came in useful when she decided that she wanted to kill the doctors. Seeing one of them drunk in the public house infuriated her. Especially when he answered his pager and she realised that he was on call. She wasn't going to risk another child suffering like Elaine had. The idiot in the Conservative Club was just as bad. Lecturing everyone on how difficult patients were. Drunk as a lord he was. Ted had thought it quite funny when she produced a brand new necktie from her handbag for each murder. It was a habit she just slipped into, carrying a necktie in her handbag – you never know when one would be required. Ted quickly took to the idea though, especially when she was particularly nice to him afterwards. Three doctors murdered, one for each year of Elaine's short life.

***

It was his bullying and drinking that finally got to her. When he wasn't shouting at her, he was on his laptop computer. Every night he got drunk on whisky. She brought him a drink whilst he was on the laptop earlier that evening. He had not even said "thank you." He had just taken the bottle from her, and had gone out to the swimming pool.

She went out to the pool several hours later. He was on the ground, unconscious. The empty bottle of whisky lay at the pool-side. She prodded him. He was in a drunken stupor. But he was heavy. It had taken a lot of effort to roll him into the swimming pool.

She walked indoors. Her arms were aching from the effort of holding him under the water. She'd leave it until the morning before she contacted the police. She picked up the kitten and sat on the stairs.

***

Getting no reply to his repeated knocking on the front door of the Williams residence, Billy Saunders wandered round to the back of the house. Jimmie Brown trailed behind him.

Jimmie looked at the extensive landscaped gardens. He stopped and looked into the ancient freshwater well.

Billy Saunders came to an abrupt halt. He was twenty yards in front of Jimmie. Billy looked at the body in the swimming pool. "Let's see if there is anyone at home."

They walked into the house through the open patio doors.

"I'll take downstairs Jimmie. You check the rest of the house."

Billy found Christine Williams sitting at the foot of the stairs. A small kitten sat at her feet. In her hand she was holding a photograph.

Billy gently took the photograph out of her hand. It was a photograph of a young couple. He turned the photograph over. "Jack and me. Chatham Town Hall dance. June 1963. The man I will marry."

***

The flicker of a computer caught Jimmie's eye as he wandered through the large house. He entered the room. Through the patio doors he could see the garden. He looked at the computer screen.

He gazed at the computer screen for a couple of minutes in a state of shock.

Putting his hand in his pocket he pulled out his wallet. He took out the bank card in the name of David Young. The sort code and account details were on there. Jimmie went to work.

Five minutes later he disconnected the computer. He picked up the laptop and walked out of the study into the garden. It took ten seconds for the laptop to hit the water at the bottom of the well.

"Jimmie, where are you?"

"Coming, I've just finished checking the rest of the house."

"We'd better inform the police. It looks as though Ted Williams got drunk and fell in the pool. His wife is in a state of shock."

CHAPTER NINETY NINE

Chatham, May 2001

Chrissie Ash stared at the gravestone. She had been back in England four weeks. She had already resumed using her maiden name. She had hated the name Christine Williams.

The Kent police had been wonderfully sympathetic over Ted's death. It came as quite a shock to her when the autopsy revealed that he was riddled with cancer and only had a few weeks to live.

She looked at the gravestone bearing the name "Edward Francis Williams."

She looked at the roses she held in her hands. She still had the roses in her hands, when she stopped at the newly dug grave at the entrance to the cemetery.

It had taken a lot of persuasion from her before Jack Watson's remains were released by the authorities. In the end they had decided that a decent burial was better than a pauper's grave.

She knelt down by the grave. "I still love you Jack." she muttered. She looked at her Timex watch. Eleven o'clock.

She still had time to visit Elaine's grave.

CHAPTER ONE HUNDRED

Inverness, May 2001

At the very moment that Chrissie Ash was talking to Jack Watson's ghost, Jimmie Brown was inserting his cash card into the cash dispenser. The card was being used for the first time. He had waited four weeks before plucking up the courage. He knew that banks had the facility to photograph users of cash machines. He just hoped that the David Young account was genuine. He hoped that the pin number was correct.

Standing beside him was a very nervous Tommy Brown.

He entered his pin number, and pressed the "balance enquiry" key. He read the figures on the screen. £2,986,045.62 Credit.

Tommy caught Jimmie as he fainted.

Tommy looked at the screen.

"You've hit the jackpot Jimmie, you've hit the jackpot."

CHAPTER ONE HUNDRED AND ONE

Inverness, January 2002

Billy Saunders looked at the brass plate on the entrance door to the suite of offices.

SAUNDERS AND BROWN
PRIVATE INVESTIGATORS

The Saunders and Brown partnership had been going three months. Billy got quite a surprise when Jimmie had put forward the idea of a detective agency. But when Jimmie produced the hard cash to back the idea Billy agreed to the proposal.

Billy had arrived for work earlier than usual that morning. An early morning call from Jimmie had advised him that visitors, a solicitor accompanied by a client accused of murder, would be at the offices by eight o'clock. "I reckon the bloke is as guilty as hell, but he wants us to investigate," had been Jimmie's observation.

"Good morning Billy. Jimmie is already in his office."

"Good morning Sheila," Billy responded.

He was still not used to seeing Sheila Jennison sitting in the receptionist chair. But even that was to change shortly when Sheila and Jimmie got married.

Billy had been at their house the previous evening.

The granny annexe was perfect for Sheila's mother.